HOME BOUND
A Survival Story

Written By
Josh Thomas

HOME BOUND

HOME BOUND

Home Bound
First Edition: August 2019
Second Edition: September 2019
Third Edition: January 2020

To my wife and kids, whom I would walk to the ends of the Earth for.

HOME BOUND

DAY 1

PROLOGUE

The early autumn sun cast long shadows across the newly cleaned cement driveway in the small suburban Michigan neighborhood. The low rumble of boat engines from Lake St. Clair could be heard from almost a mile away. The last remnants of summer fun was still trying to be claimed by the adventurous few. A warm breeze swept down the street and lifted a few scattered leaves, that had already started their descent into winter, skittering into the the dark corners of the open garage.

A lone figure stood in the open doorway and narrowed his eyes at the setting sun. He surveyed his little slice of heaven and was content. Children's laughter floated in on the warm air, echoing against the houses in his little domain. He turned his head back and forth trying to determine where it was coming from. He smiled and nodded, *of course!*. It was coming from his own back yard.

"Jake? You still out here, honey?" A warm female voice called out, pulling him out of his reverie.

"Yeah, what's up?" He turned and smiled to his wife of almost twenty years, Janey.

"If you are all done playing with your doomsday stuff, dinner's ready. Get yourself cleaned up and come and get it." She smiled and winked at him, as she turned her hips away from his gaze and headed back into the house. The movement was not lost on him. He chuckled to himself and thought, *how could I be so lucky?*

"It's not doomsday stuff, and I am not playing!" He called after her. "I am gearing up for the Scout camporee this weekend, remember?"

"Whatever, just put your stuff away and come in!" She retorted. She had always considered Jake's obsession with preparing for disaster as a "hobby". It infuriated him sometimes. Especially when it was inventory time and he would find his canned good stores were short several dozen cans. After careful checking and rechecking he would always find out later that one of the kids was having a canned food drive for the homeless at school or church,. He'd say that he didn't mind. But the truth of the matter was, he did mind. He minded a lot. He minded so much in fact that he had started a second and third stash. It meant more work for him, *better to have it and not need it, than to need it and not have it!*

He looked at the pile of camping gear he had just finished assembling together and sighed deeply. He wiped his hands on his jeans and went in.

"I was getting the totes ready for tomorrow when Joey and I have to leave. Getting it done now instead of later." He chided her.

"Yeah, yeah, sure, sure. Whatever you say Mr. Prepper." He took a deep breath and calmed himself. Deep down he hated that term, "prepper." There had been many TV shows that showcased too many crackpots and tinfoil hat wearing conspiracy nuts spouting off about the Yellowstone super volcano or an "economic collapse" or Jakes favorite, an EMP from a nuclear attack that would cause a country wide blackout! He had watched these shows with Janey and they both would deride the people on the show. But secretly, Jake was taking notes of what to do and what not to do.

"Don't call me that." He grumbled, trying to keep his feelings in check.

"I can call you whatever I want, Mr. Man!" Janey knew she had gotten under his skin, like always. She wrapped her arms around him and squeezed tightly then stood on her tiptoes and kissed him on the cheek. He instantly mellowed.

"You know, someday you will thank me!" he said.

"I know dear." She had pulled away and walked deeper into the house.

"No, really! Someday a disaster is gonna strike and you would be helpless if wasn't for me!" He pleaded after her. She casually dismissed him and his "hobby."

"Whatever you think we need, to get through whatever you think is coming, you go ahead and get it. Until then, eat!" she handed him a plate full of food and patted him on his backside, sending him on his way.

The long, oak kitchen table that doubled as a work desk both for Janey and the kids, was cleared and set for dinner. Both of his kids sat on one side bickering as they always do, but stopping when they saw their father.

"Hey Dad? Are we still camping with the scouts this weekend?" Joey asked between mouthfuls of food from his now nearly empty plate. Jake nodded in response. He marvelled at how much food his thirteen year old son could pack away. Jake smiled since it reminded him of his younger self.

"Daddy, when can I come camping with you guys?" Ella asked, her blue eyes twinkled with delight. She was two years younger than her sibling but just as adventurous and thrill seeking.

"We can go camping next weekend at Grandma's house. But if we do, then I'm gonna need some help in the garage getting your gear ready. Wanna help after dinner?"

"Yeah!"

"Good, Joey can come out and double check me on the scout stuff I already packed."

"Aw, man! Do I have to?"

"Yes, you do." Jake shut him down from further arguing with a look. Ella smiled at him lovingly.

Jake and the kids finished dinner and spent the next few hours going over sleeping bags and messkits, tents and ground pads, pocket knives and firestarters. Once the gear inspections were done, he sent them to wash and get ready for bed. It was a school night after all. He smiled as they scampered up the steps into the house and jostled to be first to the bathroom. *Youth really is wasted on the young,* he thought as he rubbed his lower back trying to rub out a kink. He followed them albeit in a little slower pace.

"Back pains?" Janey appeared from the living room, holding two glasses of wine. She held one out for him, which he gladly accepted.

"Yeah, but nothing a little massage wouldn't cure." He said, hoping his little comment wouldn't go unnoticed.

"Oh really, well you better call someone then!" she answered playfully. He looked at her, his mouth agape. After a moment he shook his head and gathered his wits.

"Ok, I will." He took out his cell phone and rapidly punched in a series of numbers and pressed the little phone symbol. He finished his wine while he waited for the party to answer. He held the phone to his ear as Janey looked on. Suddenly her phone began to vibrate in her back pocket. She smirked at him as she slid it free.

"Really?"

"Answer it," he said, setting the empty glass down next to Janey's on the coffee table.

"Ugh, fine. Hello?"

"Uh yes, hi. I was wondering if I could get a deep tissue massage."

"We don't do that here."

"Oh no, then can I get a happy ending instead?"

"You're disgusting." She said as she hung up the phone. He laughed heartily as they fell to the couch wrapped in his arms. He held her tenderly and gently kissed her cheeks and chin, slowly moving to her lips.

"You are my happy ending." He said softly. She looked deep into his eyes.

"And you're my prince charming." She answered. They kissed again, this time more deeply and without speaking rose from the couch, shut off the lights and went to the bedroom.

CHAPTER 1

The day started just like any other. The alarm went off far earlier than Jake would have liked. It was still dark out as he rubbed the sleep from his eyes. *Well, at least it's Friday*, he thought. He quietly slipped out of bed and slowly crept into the bathroom. His work schedule was such that he left the house almost a full hour before Janey, so he tried hard to make sure he didn't disturb her. He showered and then ran his fingers through his thinning dirty blond hair. *Getting old sucks,* he thought as he spied his receding hair line.

He finished grooming and dressed in silence, still mindful of his noise levels. Once he was ready to leave he softly kissed Janey on the cheek and then knelt down to pet his two golden retrievers Billie and Samantha. *My old lady*, he thought while he stroked Billie's white and caramel colored fur. She would be turning fifteen in a few weeks while his other dog, Samantha, was still the "puppy" at six years old. He glanced back at the form of his sleeping wife once more, smiled, then went to work.

He listened to the usual morning radio fodder on the way in, mostly just to keep himself awake. He switched channels frequently, just to keep from listening to those god-awful commercials about lawyers and tire companies. He paused on one station, just in time.

"Tensions are rising in the far east as North Korea's leader is quoted as saying, "The time of the West is coming to an end. The American president has insulted us for the last time." The world is now waiting anxiously for the response from the US. The North Koreans have already begun transporting it's missiles and armaments around the country and have begun negotiations with the Russian Ambassador. We will stay with this story as it develops..."

"Well, that would suck." He said to the empty truck. But it did give him some items to look into for later.

At work was where he did most of his news gathering. He tried to keep abreast of the goings on in the world while trying to maintain some security in his own private one. The headlines were enough to give a grown man nightmares. If you knew what to look for that is:

North Korea Forces Building In The South
U.S. Bombers Start 24 Hour A Day Patrol Missions
China Diplomats Pulled Out Of North Korean Capital
U.S. Troops Recalled From Leave

President Tweets Disrespect About Leader of N. K.
Prices of Hot Dogs Rise For Sixth Straight Month
This can't be good. He read what he could, and bookmarked the rest for later perusal. He was thankful it was Friday.

Friday isn't too bad of a workday in Jake's line of work, but sometimes it could be pretty busy. That day was not one of the busy ones. Late September was slow for the business that Jake was in, as a Systems Administrator he pretty much waited on the programmers upstairs to ask for something. The tried and true, hurry up and wait philosphy and methodology. He maintained the software programs for them, while they mucked them up a good bit.

Before Jake realized it lunch time had rolled around. Ernie, his boss of only seven years, walked up to Jake's cube as he always did.

"Lunchtime! Any choices of destination?" Ernie was what some might call elderly, he had been working in the IT field for about 30 years, so he had done and seen it all. Suddenly a silver haired head popped up above the cube wall, across from Jake.

"Red Olive!" Todd said. Todd, was a co-worker and colleague of Jake's

"Again? Didn't we have that last week?" Jake sighed. "You guys go on without me, I might just hang back here, you know. Raid the vending machines."

"Okee-dokiee!" Todd and Ernie turned and headed for the door.

"DING DING DING"

"BZZT, BZZT, BZZT"

"DINGLE-DEE, DINGLE-DEE, DINGLE-DEE"

Jake's, and seemingly everyone else's, phones started ringing or vibrating. The sound was discordant and chaotic since not everyone had the same notification sound for an incoming text message. Jake looked down at his phone as did everyone else. *How can we all get a text message at the same time?* he thought. The message was short but clear.

Emergency Alert

A NUCLEAR BALLISTIC MISSILE THREAT INBOUND TO U.S. SEEK IMMEDIATE SHELTER. THIS IS NOT A DRILL.

Voices suddenly pierced the silence. Panic and hysteria all at once.

"Is this some sort of joke?"

"Where did this come from?"

"I need to call my wife!"

"What is this?"

Jake looked at his phone and immediately grabbed his mobile HAM radio walkie-talkie unit. He was also a short range amateur radio operator in his spare time. Jake brought it to work with him everyday. Mostly just to listen to the local radio stations. He quickly disconnected the battery pack and tossed them both into his work backpack. Fearing the worst, he snatched his water bottle and empty pop bottle from his desk, ran to the kitchen area, filled them and tossed both into his backpack. People were starting to wonder what to do, some had begun crying, some were furiously trying to call their loved ones. *Maybe I should call Janey?* He thought. *No, the phone networks are probably flooded. A text? Maybe.* He fired off a quick text:

I love you, I am coming for you, stay there/seek shelter. –J. He stabbed his finger on the SEND icon and hoped for the best.

It shows as delivered, hopefully she would see it and know what to do. Maybe she would see it on her fitbit. These thoughts and more raced through his head. People were crying now, and some were hiding under their desks.

Would it be a high-altitude detonation? That could trigger an EMP blast, but if it was a direct impact detonation, then it would depend on the target. Detroit? Nah, no value. That nuclear power plant down in Monroe? That was more plausible. He raced back to his desk, Ernie and Todd had come back in and were staring at their phones as well.

11

They were discussing what to do when they watched Jake grab his coat and leave his laptop.

"Jake? Where are you going? What do you know?" It was Ernie.

"Ernie, Todd, Good luck and godspeed, I am leaving. You should too." He shook their hands firmly.

"But if this is true and a missile hits..." His voices trailed off, Todd was looking at Ernie and Jake clearly concerned for his well-being.

"I don't think a missile will strike anywhere near us. In fact, I think it will be a high-altitude detonation. An EMP will knock out all of our cars, and computers. Go now while you can!" Jake turned and started running for the door but before he could reach it, the overhead lights flickered and darkened. Voices, once quietly skirting the edges of panic, now cried out in one cacophonous wall of sound. *Damn it! I hate being right.* Jake looked back to Todd and Ernie, they slowly raised their hands and waved goodbye. Jake returned the gesture, left the building and made for his now lifeless truck.

Outside, the weather was nice and calm, not in any way letting on to the terror that everyone was now feeling and facing. People had begun to stream out of the two story office building. Some were looking up into the sky, straining to see a missile or projectile. Others expected to see a gigantic mushroom cloud. Many others were running for their cars and trucks, frantically pressing the unlock button on their keyfobs, oblivious to the fact that they were now dead. Jake shook his head as he pulled his keys from his pocket.

He ran to his truck, a dark red Ford F-150, which he strategically parked the furthest from the building and had backed in. Behind the truck was a dense urban forest that hid a short trail. Jake had walked the trail many times for exercise and knew that it was part of a municipal park.

He jammed the key into the door and twisted. Hearing the familiar clunk of the lock unlocking the door, he flung it open and dumped the contents of his work bag onto the seat. He unzipped the largest pocket and dumped out the water bottles, his walkie talkie with battery and his "Emergency Lunch", (two protein bars and a rice krispy treat). He searched through the rest of the truck and found a few meager camping supplies, a magnesium bar and scraper (a small piece of hacksaw blade), another folding pocket knife and his vehicle first-aid kit. He transfered the now precious commodities into his GHB.

His GHB, or Get-Home bag was just that. A bag or pack designed to get one from where ever they were to home. In this case, it was packed with a few days of food and water, a change of clothes, a tarp for shelter, multiple devices to start a fire, a mess kit and various other odds and ends to help a person get home. Janey had scoffed at the idea of the Get–Home Bag, especially since Jake spent good money on it!

He took off his light fleece office coat, attached it to the bag and then lifted the whole pack onto his back. He quickly moved to the back of the truck, and dropped the tailgate. Peering into the darkness, he grabbed his scout hiking stick. It was a gift from a friend at summer camp last year, a five-foot long piece of hickory, stained and sealed against the weather, with a length of paracord for a handwrap. *Maps! Don't forget the maps!* Reaching back into the cab, Jake pulled out a manilla envelope with a series of maps that he had printed out. These maps detailed a way to get home. *STOP AND LOOK!* He berated himself internally. He knew that he tended to get panicky and rushed when in a hurry. Knowing this weakness he had to tell himself to stop and look for anything else that he might be missing. After one last look at the truck and building he took a deep breath and thought, *Here we go!* He turned and trudged into the forest.

Well, according to my planning and what I have read, I can expect people to really lose their shit in about 2-3 days, which coincidently is the amount of time it will take me to get home. Great. Checking the map, Jake had calculated that it will be twenty-four and half miles of walking just to get to Morgan Hills, where Janey was employed. That worked out to about eight hours of walking, non-stop. He knew that he will have to stop for food and bathroom breaks, so realistically it could be anywhere from nine to ten hours. *Not good enough, he thinks. I knew I should have invested in a folding bike or something to make this trip quicker. Maybe I can "appropriate" one along the way? Something to think about on the way home. First stop: Janey!*

He took his first steps into the woods towards home. Far above him a large metal cylinder hurtled through the sky. It's target was programmed into it's internal computer. The one hundred and fifty kiloton nuclear device primed as it streaked over Jake. The missile hurtled through the atmosphere, struck it's target and detonated in fire and fury. The triple cylinder skyscraper that was the headquarters for a worldwide automobile manufacturer was no more. The flash from the bomb lit up the sky in every direction and was brighter than the sun. The fireball burned everything in a half mile radius, buildings, vehicles, animals and people. All gone. The mushroom cloud climbed high into the sky, igniting fear in the hearts of all who saw it.

Jake emerged from the small woods and looked south. He fell to the ground and prayed.

CHAPTER 2

Being a chemist, or more accurately, a chemical lab technician was tedious work. Janey stood at the countertop running another set of tests on another set of samples, *just like the good monkey that I am*, she thought derisively. She had worked at her job for almost eighteen years and was pretty much in the same place as when she started.

The management had been the only thing that changed. Her current boss was a real piece of work. Francis Hurley, AIC. Asshole in Charge. *At least it's Friday and we have nothing planned for the weekend*, she thought. *Maybe I can just sit and relax, maybe go to Annie's with the kids and go swimming.* Annie was her sister who lived a few miles away from Janey and Jake. *Ooh, I'll stop and get some Sangria mix and call Annie on the way home. We could make a day out of it, and oh shit!* She spied a familiar figure enter the lab.

Francis came into the lab. Again. He liked to come in and hover over his staff. It made them all really nervous. In the past they had tried to engage him in some minor conversation but he either ignored them or disregarded anything they thought was important.

Francis was a new hire from an outside agency. The higher ups deemed it necessary to hire new blood to try and invigorate the staff. Apparently there was an accountant or two that was monitoring the lab's statistics and felt that they weren't completing enough work. So to alleviate that, they reassigned Janey's old boss and gave them Francis.

He would assign a project to a technician and once that project was completed he would berate that person for not doing it the way he would have done it! It didn't matter what the difference was, the outcome was the same! The project was completed successfully, but because it wasn't done HIS way, that employee wouldn't get a raise that year. Some real douchbaggery going on there.

Now he was back in the lab, surveying his team. He turned and walked towards Janey. She tried not to let him get to her, but it wasn't working. She started trembling slightly, the pipette in her hand was moving so much that she was having a problem properly dosing out the sample to the solution for testing. Francis stopped at her station and watched. The protocol called for exactly six drops of sample to the premeasured solution for testing. In her shaking she had added eight or more drops, ruining the sample and solution.

"Why can't you properly work that pipette, Janey? It is one of the simplest of devices in our lab? Maybe I should assign you to the fume hood and cleaning stations. Do you think you could screw that up as well?" His douchebaggery knew no bounds.

"Sorry Francis. I, I, I didn't mean to.", she stammered, "I was startled. It won't happen again." She was on the verge of tears. Again. She hated him for his constant beratement of her. He didn't seem to do that to anyone else, just her. He stood there glaring at her for what felt like an eternity, finally he turned and walked to the door. He reached out with one hand to push it open, but before his palm touched the silver rectangle of shiny stainless steel, it opened! Chris, one of Janey's co-workers and good friend, came through the open doorway. She paused long enough to look Francis up and down, saw his outstretched hand and gave it a hard slap!

"How ya doin, Frankie?" She smiled and walked passed him. In shock and revulsion he produced a small bottle of hand sanitizer and began cleaning his hands. He muttered under his breath about being called Frankie, as he stormed out of the lab.

"What's with him?" Chris asked.

"I don't know, I do know that he is being an asshole, again." She had stopped trembling and was regaining her composure.

"Want to go to lunch?"

"I guess, oh, wait. I can't. Francis gave us bunch of samples to re-run because he wasn't satisfied with the results."

"Tell that ass-hat to run them himself!" Chris didn't work with Francis. She was assigned to another department.

"I can't do that!" she shot back. Chris saw the fear in her eyes.

"Ok then. Hey, don't let him get to you. He is all bark and no bite!" Chris tried to cheer her up, but it was having no effect. Janey just shrugged and went back to her samples.

"Sorry, I can't go with you, if I don't get these samples done, then I won't be able to leave on time, and then Jake will get pissy because I have to stay late. Go have fun and I'll see you later." She waved to Chris and went back to her work.

I hate this place and that dickhead Francis! She thought. Her mind wandered to thoughts of home and the kids. *Ugh! I have to get Ella some new dance shoes sometime this week, and plan a Girl Scout meeting for Thursday, and Ella has gymnastics tonight. I need to text Jake and see if he can take her tonight, I don't think I will be out early enough. The house is a mess and the dogs are due for their yearly checkup. So much to do.*

She stuck her head back under the the fume hood to start another batch of testing, when her wrist vibrated. She tried to read the scrolling text but it was too fast for her to read fully. *Did that say something about a missile strike? What is going on? Is this a joke Jake? I don't find this funny at all!* She thought she could hear voices out in the hall, but with all of the noise of the fans above her, she shrugged it off, now mad at Francis AND Jake. She scowled and went back to her work. Again her wrist vibrated and this time she looked at it right away. It was from Jake:

I love you, I am coming for you, stay there-J

BZZT! ZAP! POP!

The lab was suddenly plunged into absolute darkness. It was an interior room with no skylights or windows. *Strange, the emergency lights haven't kicked on. I wish I was back in my old lab, at least the sunlight would be coming through the windows.* Outside the lab she could hear voices now that the fans had ceased spinning. Usually there were indicator lights of varying intensity on the front of the scanners and microscopes and Ion-Chromatography machines. Now there was nothing. The voices in the hallway were growing in intensity. The door burst open, flooding the lab with light. Janey shielded her eyes against the bright light..

"JANEY! YOU IN HERE?" Chris had come back and was yelling for her.

"Yes I am, Chris. What's going on? I just got a text from Jake saying to stay here and that he is coming for me? And something about a missile?"

"You don't know? Didn't you get the text? Everyone else did?"

"What text? Francis doesn't allow our cell phones in the lab, because our personal conversations take away from precious lab time."

"I can't remember all of it, but it said that there was something about a nuclear missile inbound and to seek shelter!"

"WHAT!?!?" Janey could hardly believe her ears. Images of mushroom clouds and her husband and kids in danger flashed through her mind.

"Yeah, couldn't this the be same thing that happened in Hawaii a few months ago?" Chris was trying to work it through. Janey looked at her friend for few moments.

"Wait, they didn't lose power. We did. Check your phone!" Chris held hers out for both to see. They both looked at the dark screen, now just a really expensive paperweight.

They stood in silence for a few moments, while other technicians streamed out of the other labs. They asked about the phone messages and what was happening.

"EVERYONE ON MY TEAM, TO THE CONFERENCE ROOM RIGHT NOW!" Francis had appeared at the end of the corridor and was bellowing to the throng of people no gathered there. The rest of Janey's co-workers, Jiang-Li, Mike, Chris and Randy had gathered together in the hallway and were frantically trying their personal electronic devices. Everyone was relatively calm, but there was some panic. Most heard Francis's announcement so they all went to the conference room. Those that didn't report to Francis went as well to hear what he had to say, hoping for some good news.

Lab technicians, sales staff, secretaries, maintenance staff, and loading dock workers all tried to jam into the conference room. Janey, Jiang-Li, and Mike had all made it into the room and could barely hear each other it was so loud.

"I think someone hit a power pole"

"A car accident you think?"

"How could a car accident or a down pole make our laptops shutdown?"

"I thought I heard thunder, maybe a substation was hit?"

"Then why are our phones not working?"

"I don't think this is localized to our building, look outside!" Those that heard this comment, turned to look out the windows onto MacMillan Highway.

MacMillan Highway was a four lane boulevard that ran north and south parallel to the interstate. It ran from 12 Mile road all the way to M-89, about eight miles in total. Usually it was a non-stop thoroughfare of vehicles. Tractor trailers, pickup trucks and cars all used it as a service drive of sorts to bypass the interstate. Now it was a parking lot. Drivers that had the wherewithall, had pulled off into parking lots or side streets, the rest let their vehicles come to rest in the middle of the lanes. Some were not so lucky. Right out the window the employees could see a tractor trailer with a huge pizza company logo painted on the side of the trailer. Black smoke billowed out from under it. Wedged underneath the trailer was a small white car, that looked like it was pushed there by a large blue pickup truck. The driver of the tractor had gotten out and was looking under the trailer, and at the truck. The pickup truck driver wasn't moving, the evidence of injury was splattered on the inside of the windshield. There was no movement from the what was left of the car either. Just smoke and flames poured from the interior of the car. Janey craned her neck to look further down the road. Dark plumes of smoke could be seen rising from the nearest intersections. Car fires. More accidents. More death. Some of the employees began to cry.

Ted Shellon, head of the building maintenance team finally made his way to the front of the room.

"EVERYONE QUIET DOWN! WOULD EVERYONE PLEASE QUIET DOWN!" He was waving his arms, trying to get the attention of everyone and get them to stop talking. It had the desired effect.

"Thank you. We will be closing the building effective immediately. We do not know what happened. Some of you may have received a text message about an incoming nuclear missile. We believe that this was sent in error. Just like that incident in Hawaii earlier this year. Please gather your belongings and go home."

All at once there was shouting, screaming, and crying out.

"Ted, what if we can't get home?"

"I ride the bus, what if the busses aren't working?"

"My kids! Does anyone have a working cell phone?"

Bill Shannon, a scumbag, obnoxious salesman that Janey has had the unfortunate encounter or two with, looked around at the gathered throng. He had been sitting next to Janey and had been impulsively running his hands through his greasy, black hair.

"You all can suck it, I plan on driving out of here in my brand new electric Tesla sportscar!"

"With what power?" Janey asked. He looked at her and sneered, then got up and began pushing and shoving his way to the door.

"Get out of the way, you assholes, I'm outta here! Get out of my freaking way!" More employees fled from the conference room. The large group quickly dwindled down to just Janey, Jiang-Li, and Mike. They sat together in shock, trying to process what was just said to them. Janey remembered Jake's text about him coming for her and to stay put. *Could it be true? Maybe I should try to go too! Jake will realize I left and meet me at home! What about the kids? They are at school, they will have some procedures in place, won't they?* Just as she was about to get up and leave, Francis stepped into the room.

"Ok team, here is what we are going to do. Get your stuff from your office and come back here in ten minutes. We can get some paperwork done and then you can be free to leave at three PM."

"Are you serious?" Mike asked.

"Yes, why? Are you thinking of leaving, Mike? Just know that if you do, you will not be welcome back."

Mike stared at him, mentally trying to understand how someone could be so callous and obtuse.

"Fine, piss off Francis! I am outta here. He turned back to his two co-workers. "You should go too!" Mike looked at them and then back to Francis, flipped him the bird and left.

"Fine. Leave. Looks like we will have a position opening up for another lab technician!"

Janey had finally snapped out of her stupor and glared at Francis. *If this is the end of the world, then I will be waiting for Jake to come for me. In the meantime, I'll play nice, for now.* She looked at him again. *Asshole.*

CHAPTER 3

Oh God, this pack is heavy, he thought. *Keep going, it will get lighter and I will get stronger.* He knew that most of the weight was from the water. Thinking of the clear water sloshing around in their containers had now made him thirsty. Again. *Great, now I am thirsty! I just stopped ten minutes ago, I can't stop for another twenty!* The mushroom cloud had dissipated and it looked to be heading east over Canada. He thanked the Lord for that. He was making good time according to his map and pace. He checked his map and saw that he had already made it north to Eleven Mile road and east to Halestead in about an hour. *I'm glad I packed my puffer! These first four miles are already wearing me down! I better slow my pace a bit.* His puffer was a rescue style inhaler. *Exercise induced asthma is a bitch,* he thought. Stopping for a moment, he dug out his inhaler, took two puffs and put it in an easier to reach pocket. He reshouldered his pack and trudged on.

He had been gone from work just over two hours and had traversed 4 miles, through a park and down vehicle clogged roadways. He had seen many people milling about their cars and trucks, quite a few people fighting because of a minor traffic accident and a couple of injured people walking around in a daze. Jake assumed it was from shock or a concussion. So far no one had tried to talk to Jake or even acknowledge that he was there. Which was exactly what he hoped for. *Just blend in, move quickly and quietly* he thought. There had only been one instance of looting that Jake witnessed.

Outside a gas station, a group of youths ran from the store front with cartons and cartons of cigarettes in their arms. They ran past Jake, who was going in the opposite direction, with an Arabian man running after them, presumably the shop keeper. He was shouting in a language that Jake didn't understand, nor care to at the moment. He took a quick moment to check his maps and he saw that he was close to a golf course. *I should be there in an hour or so. Rest stop ahead!*

Feathering Hills Golf Club appeared out of the haze that Jake hoped was early evening and not any fallout from the initial attack. The golf club's lush rolling hills and carefully manicured fairways led to equally trimmed and maintained greens. Some of which were encircled by dark, blue water hazards. Jake could imagine himself playing a round or two here with his brothers and father. *In a different time and world maybe.* He was still very close to his brothers, but his father had passed away seven years ago from lung cancer. It doesn't matter how much you plan, there were some things you just can't plan for.

"FORE!" Jake looked up in time to avoid an errant golf ball slice the air in front of him. *What the hell? There are people still golfing? Didn't they see the text alert? Probably not as they are on the course, but that was almost four hours ago!*

Some people found it to be quite rude to have your cell phone with you on the course as it could disrupt the other players. Jake always had his with him, just in case. Except now it was useless.

"Sorry, young fella! I pulled that last one little bit!" An elderly gentleman with a shock of blazing white hair crested a small hill and was pulling his clubs behind him in a rolling cart. He smiled warmly at Jake and shrugged apologetically.

"Excuse me, sir, but why are you golfing? At a time like this?!" Jake asked him incredulously.

"What are you talking about son? Do you mean that text message hub bub? Bah! Just like the sixties with Kennedy and the Bay of Pigs. It don't mean anything." He had already pulled out his next club and was practicing his swing for the shot.

"Excuse me again, sir. You do understand that we have been attacked? An EMP or maybe a nuclear bomb? No working electronics?" He was dumbfounded by this man's behavior and attitude.

"Good! Take us back to the olden times. That's what this country needs anyway. A reset, or a uh, what do you kids call it? Ah! A do-over!" He swung the club and managed to put the ball on the green.

Jake thought about it all the time. The way things were going, the country, hell, the whole world needed a reset.

"I agree, but shouldn't you be home with your wife or kids or grandkids?" Jake was getting worked up at this perfect stranger and how he just didn't seem to care.

"Well, now see, Margie passed on just last year, and my kids all live out of state with their kids. I am too old to do what it looks like you are doing, so I am doing what I love. If this is the way it is to be, then so be it." He was content to meet his maker on his own terms. Jake understood.

"My apologies sir. I am sorry. I didn't know." He felt ashamed.

"Oh, no worries fella. I've been through a lot worse than this and believe you me, the good ole, U. S. of A. will come out of it!" Spoken like a true veteran of the armed forces.

"Take care of yourself son!" he waved and walked away. Jake bid him farewell and moved off to an out of the way spot under a large tree. He was amazed at the old man's cavalier attitude, but then again, that man was much older and probably lived a long and full life. Where as Jake was still young, in his prime and ready to live. That man was probably ready to die, and was doing what he loved to do.

He plunked himself down under the large boughs of a maple tree and quickly emptied one of the water bottles. He dug through his pack and pulled out a protein bar. Satisfied that he had refueled himself he glanced at his Get Home Bag. *I should take quick stock of my supplies again. I haven't checked this pack in awhile.* He opened the pack and started making a mental checklist of items. *I have a Sawyer water filter and an empty water bladder. Score!* He checked his watch and noted the time. He saw the skinny little hand slowly tick of the seconds. Looking at his watch he smiles, *thank God I have my Invicta! I know that once I get home, my 2 others and my Seiko automatics will be given to Janey, and Joey.*

His watch collection will finally be important to Janey now! His watches were automatic not quartz, which means that all he needs to do to wind them was shake them or wear them. A small counterweight spun inside them and wound a spring. No need for batteries! He lifted the empty water bottle and bladder out of the pack. *I need to find some more water to refill my pack.* He stowed the empty bottle, and policed his trash up. Again he lifted the pack onto his back and looked around. He spied a small trash receptacle near a tee box.

31

He made his way over and dropped his waste in it. Usually there were water jugs at the tee boxes. He quickly glanced around this one and found no such jug. However he saw a rudimentary map of the current hole. A two hundred and ninety-five yard par four with two sand traps in front of the green, but what intrigued Jake the most was the small blue oval just past the tee box. A water hazard. *There are water hazards on the course…hmm,* he thought as he rubbed his chin.

CHAPTER 4

Janey started to think about what was happening, just like with Jake, the people around her said that their electronics didn't work. She vaguely remembered something Jake said about EMP's and electronics.

"Oh, shit", she said. She went looking for Chris, and found her in the market room and asked for her help.

"Sure, what for?" Chris said.

"I want to go out to my car and I think the building door locks won't be working since we have no power. They would be physically locked and the badge readers won't be working. So I need you to hold the doors for me."

"Oh, yeah. Okay. Let's go."

People had been leaving the building like rats leaving a sinking ship. Janey was now praying that there isn't a nuclear missile heading right for her.

While out in the parking lot, she saw many people trying to unlock or start their cars but with no success. She saw Bill Shannon standing outside his car furiously pressing the unlock button on his fob and clearly not understanding why the car door won't unlock.

Janey walked by him, to her own car, and discreetly pushed the unlock button, just as Bill did. The car remained locked. Panic started to rush over her, but she quickly pushed it back. She turned the key fob over and slid out the emergency access key. Carefully and discreetly, she manually unlocked the door. She looked back at him, *an emergency access key, does your Tesla have that feature, asshat?* Bill watched her open her car with her fob in her hand, not understanding about the access key. Then the lightbulb finally clicked. He fumbled with the fob, twisting and turning it over in a desperate search for the key. His shoulders slumped in defeat as he realized that his car doesn't have such a key. Janey smirked as she grabbed the bag Jake had packed for her and ran back into the building.

The reality of the situation finally started to creep into her mind. *Jake is in Livonia, I am here in Morgan Hills, and the kids are at school! My mom is in Chesterfield and then Annie is GOD knows where. What the hell am I gonna do! Holy shit!* The enormity of the situation was pressing down on her. Her mind and heart weighed heavily as she started to break down. Tears streamed down her face and she openly started to cry. Chris and Jiang-Li attempted to comfort her.

"Jiang-Li, grab her backpack and follow me." She helped Janey to her feet and they guided her back to the conference room. Janey fell into one of the chairs. She buried her face in her hands and wept. She wept for Chris and Jiang-Li, and Mike and Ted. *I wish I had listened to Jake more!*

"Janey, are you ok?" A soft and tiny voice broke her out of her pity party. She looked up into the warm smile of her often silent co-worker, Jiang-Li. Janey sniffled and wiped her nose. She smiled at her friend and nodded.

Chris had opened the bag and found a piece of paper on top.

"Janey, there is a note from Jake." Chris said softly. She handed the note to Janey and she read it once, then again, and finally out loud to her friends.

"Janey stay put, I am coming for you. Take the supplies in the bag and ration them to stay alive. I will try to contact you over the radio I have put in this bag. Hopefully it still works if it was an EMP. I AM coming for you and I should be there in less than 24 hours. Love Jake"

She felt calmer after reading his message. Snippets of talks and bits of conversations with him flooded her. Discussions where he tried telling her that he had wanted them to be prepared, being involved in Scouting does that to a person.

Jake had been involved in their son's scouting career ever since Joey was a cub scout in the first grade. Jake started out just being an involved parent, to now running the Boy Scout Troop as the Scoutmaster. Be Prepared is their motto and Jake tried to get her to see it. *I let him do it,* she always thought. Now she was so glad he did.

Francis was getting irritated. He had been watching the women get the bag and Janey's emotional breakdown. That was not what bothered him. He had watched this whole drama play out and no one was doing their work!

"Janey, Jiang-Li, what is the meaning of this! Are you on a break? I expected you both to be working on your reports!" He tried to sound important. Janey glared at him, her eyes narrowing to tiny slits.

"PISS OFF, FRANCIS!" She screamed at him. The sudden outburst startled them all. His eyes flew wide in astonishment, no one had ever spoken to him that way. He quickly turned and left. That definitely made her feel better. Jiang-Li and Chris stared at her, mouths hanging ajar. Janey looked back at them.

"Close your mouths, you're attracting flies." They all bust out laughing at that. All except Francis.

=================== * ===================

A couple of hours had gone by, and Janey had regained her composure while everyone else was losing their minds. Jiang-Li had become more withdrawn than normal. Most of the building was empty now. With the exception of Francis's team, almost everyone had vacated the premises. The stress had finally started to penetrate Francis. He was freaking out because he didn't know what to do, or who to contact to for help. All of the directors and management above him worked offsite. There was no power and no phones so he couldn't call anyone. Most of the remaining employees had congregated in the break room. Three large skylights installed above the seating area illuminated the room quite well. He could take it no more.

"I don't think you people understand the seriousness of the situation! We have reports that need to be filled out and samples to be logged! We should be working!" He was pacing back and forth, from wall to wall. He was supposed to be charge, but everyone was ignoring him.

"Why is no one listening to me! I know you can hear me!" HELLO?!? That's it! I am writing you all up for insubordination and these will go into your personnel files for review!" They all just stared at him, no one cared and some even left the room. He threw his hands into the air and left the break room heading for his office.

Chris, Jiang-Li and Janey were all sitting together since the rest of the chemists and sales staff had left the building.

"What should we do? Is there someplace we could go?" Jiang-Li asks. Janey looked back to the doorway making sure that Francis was truly gone.

"Jiang-Li, my husband is coming for me. So I need to stay here, as sucky as that sounds. I know that when he gets here, he will know what to do. We have a saying in our family, "What's the plan, man?" He always has a plan."

"Guys, since I live sorta close by, I just might try to walk home." Chris said. She was thinking of her own husband and four year old daughter. He worked from home and provided day care for their daughter.

"Chris, are you sure? I would like it if you could stay with me until Jake gets here. Only until tomorrow." Janey asked.

"Honey, I would but I am worried about Maddie and Daniel. I've wanted to go ever since this started. I can't wait any longer, I'm sorry kiddo." She hugged Janey then Jiang-Li, and waved goodbye.

"I am worried too. My family is good to me too." Jiang-Li said in somewhat okay English. Being Chinese could have it's advantages and disadvantages. Mandarin was her first language, English was a distant second.

"Yeah, Jiang-Li. I am worried about my family too, but I have faith that Jake will get here and we can get my kids, together." She said a quick prayer for Jake's safety and speedy arrival.

CHAPTER 5

Darkness had begun to descend upon Jake. The suburbs were alive with activity, which made him think that these folks had no freaking clue what was going on. Through the trees and shrubs that line the properties of the neatly manicured lawns, he saw many people out in their backyards cooking on their grills. Blissfully unaware that the worst was yet to come. The smell of hamburgers and steaks, fish and hotdogs wafted through the air. *Better to cook that stuff now, while the smell isn't so appealing to those who don't have any. Best to use the meat before it goes bad.* These thoughts and more ran rampant through his mind as he trudged on.

The houses closest to the street were lit from within by candles and fireplaces. The low roar of generators could be heard in the distance. *What a waste, using up the gas now when it will be in high demand later.* The running generators were a good sign. Maybe the EMP didn't take everything out. His mind flashed back to all the literature he had been devouring over the past few years. How to protect your gear from an EMP by putting it in a metal trash can lined with chicken wire and a styrofoam block! Rubbish.

No one really knew what the effects of an EMP would have on todays technology. The department of defense had run simulations based on the little amount of data gathered during the Los Almos testing in the mid '40s during World War II and then again in the early '60s.

Back in the early 1940s when Dr. Robert Oppenheimer and his Manhattan Project team members built and tested the first two atomic bombs there was a spike in the electromagnetic interference at the time of detonation. But back then all, if not most, electronic circuitry was vacuum tubes and switches. The effect was registered on the equipment but the impact was insignificant and was thought to be due to the radiation and nothing else.

The closest the world had come to an actual EMP disaster was July ninth in the year 1962. The United States Atomic Energy Commission and the Pentagon had conducted a series of nuclear and hydrogen bomb tests over the Pacific Ocean from their base on Johnston Island. The island sat 500 nautical miles southwest of Hawaii. It was thought that that was a safe enough distance from a habitable island.

One of the tests was given the codename Starfish Prime. The test was designed to test if a nuclear warhead that was detonated high in the atmosphere could destroy an incoming Soviet Union missiles.

The first two tests were utter failures, one was destroyed seconds after launch and the other exploded on the launch pad. Both failures resulted in massive nuclear fallout upon the launch site and testing facility.. The third test however, was a success, from a certain point of view.

The warhead sat atop a Thor missile that was launched and had performed flawlessly, delivering it's nuclear payload into space. The 1.4 megaton warhead detonated approximately 240 miles above the surface of the Pacific Ocean. That's when all hell broke loose. The aurora from the blast could be seen as far east as Hawaii and as far south as New Zealand. The effects were felt almost immediately. Streetlights blew out, circuit breakers tripped, telephone services crashed, aircraft radios malfunctioned and burglar alarms sounded.

Scientists and the military were stunned by the results of Starfish Prime. They had known about the EMP but the effects of the blast far exceeded their expectations. Despite the very public detonation of the weapon, the cause of the power failures and municipal utilities malfunctions remained secret for years. Conspiracy theorists and the doomsayers however have been documenting and discussing this since then, how a single nuclear weapon might be used to cripple the

United States of America in one blow. Jake knew that it wasn't a question of how, but when.

In today's world a cell phone could be disrupted from a strong refrigerator magnet! In all of Jake's planning he knew that there was only so much that could be planned for. He planned for the actual disasters that could befall him and his family. Tornados, blizzards, floods, and severe thunderstorms were at the top of that list. All natural disasters for his geographic area. He hadn't really planned for any man-made disasters.

He had read an interesting article put out by FEMA, the Federal Emergency Management Agency. It stated that if a nuclear bomb was detonated above the middle of America, then the EMP would effect any electronic circuits connected to a power source from Philadelphia, PA to San Fransisco, CA. It was an interesting point that Jake had tucked away in the back of his mind. But it was something that crept up to the forefront every so often. Sometimes it wasn't even a conscious thought. He had gotten into the habit of unplugging certain devices. His HAM radio was one, sitting on his desk in the basement office. *My radio!* Jake stopped and dropped his pack, rifled though it and pulled out his small hand held radio that he had brought with him to work. He had disconnected the battery before the pulse, but with renewed hope he jammed the battery pack back into the rear of the radio and held his breath as he turned it on.

*CLICK. Nothing but a soft hiss of static was coming from the small speaker. A sense of relief washed over him as he quickly scanned the local frequencies, searching for a familiar voice or sound. He was terrified that it too was dead. With some trepidation he keyed the mic.

"CQ, CQ, CQ. This is KE8ITZ, is anyone out there?" He waited a few beats before trying again.

"This is KE8ITZ, is anyone there?" Nothing. He switched frequencies to the one he had set on Janey's radio. Hers was a simple department store radio, part of a set of two that were really used for short range communications. It could pick up Jake's transmissions, but he wouldn't be able to hear her response because her radio was of a lower wattage. He keyed the mic again.

"Janey, this is Jake, if you can hear this I am okay and I am on my way. ETA should be 0800 tomorrow morning. I'll try again in a few hours. I love you. KE8ITZ, Clear." He released the button and took a deep breath to steady his nerves. After a few minutes of silence he turned the radio off to conserve power, and stowed it back in his pack. He hefted the pack up and onto his shoulders and pushed off to continue his trek. Hearing the generators in the nearby neighborhood gave him hope. *Maybe FEMA was right for a change*, he thought.

He continued walking past the enticing smell of hotdogs and hamburgers, and past the laughing and smiling faces of families that were together. He wondered if they knew what was really happening to the world around them. The thought of his own family, scattered like so many leaves on the wind, gave him the drive to continue. Janey was stuck at the one place that she didn't want to be, twelve miles away while the kids were stuck at their school, forty miles away.

Just as the last rays of the sun dipped below the horizon, he glimpsed a sign up ahead. Inglenook Park. *Great, I made it thirteen and a half miles in five and half hours! Not bad. Not great, but not horrible.* This was the place he had planned to stop and rest for the night in case he had to walk home. He quickly scanned around for an area to set up his camp. *There!* Nestled past a darkened barn and a playground was a dense stand of trees and bushes thick with vegetation. *An oasis! Hopefully it's undisturbed and unoccupied,* he thought as he trotted over to it.

Darkness was falling fast as he searched for a spot to hunker down for the night. Finding a perfectly secluded spot behind some thicker bushes and under a small pine tree, he dropped his pack. The boughs of the tree provided a perfect roof to protect him from any unscheduled weather or dew, while the bushes hid him from any prying eyes that could be spying from the street. He pulled the dark green survival tarp from his pack and wrapped it around him. He made sure that the silver mylar was on the inside to reflect his body heat back to his body. He set the pack behind him and tried to get comfortable.

Just as he closed his eyes and started to relax, his eyes flashed open. He could hear voices in the dark, unfamiliar and unfriendly sounding. He could make out two or three different pitches, more than one definitely. Not rural sounding either, definitely urban, inner-city. *Great! A bunch of thugs, and all I have is a folding knife. It's a good knife, but if they have a gun or a bunch of guns, then I might be screwed.* Laying on the ground gave him the advantage. He could see through the bushes just a bit and in the sparse moonlight he could see a pair of neon yellow sneakers. They stood out pretty good in the darkness. *Must be coated in reflective material,* he thought. The shoes were moving closer and closer it wasn't long before he could hear the voices clearly.

"Shit, man, which way did he go?"

"Did you see that backpack that muthafucka was carryin wit him? Might be somethin in it worth takin for ourselves!"

"Gots to be some good shit in there!"

"Yeah, and he's in OUR neighborhood now bro and that pack is as good as ours!"

"Shut up! You stupid assholes, he's prolly listening to us right now!" The voice sounded deeper, more commanding and Jake swore that it came from the owner of the Yellow sneakers. *He must be their leader*, Jake thought. They were almost on top of him now, only standing a short distance away from the bushes.

"Hey T, what if he ain't give it up?"

"We drop his ass and take it! HA haha!" They all laughed as they turned and continued searching the park. *Well shit! Guess I'm not sleeping tonight.*

Thoughts about relocating to a safer spot or possibly walking through the night played out in his mind. Slowly and carefully he re-adjusted his position. *Ouch!* He turned his head and saw that he had been stabbed by a long, skinny and very sharp looking thorn. As his eyes focused he could see hundreds of thorns on the branches and twigs above and around him. Smiling, he thanked the Lord for small favors. If the thugs were to see him there, they would have to go around the trees to find the spot that he had used to gain access to the safe center.

Thirty minutes later he could barely hear their foot falls and snickering conversation. *God I wish I had some night vision goggles!* The sounds of the thugs faded and a few hours later he drifted off to a restless sleep

KABLAM! KABLAM! KABLAM! Jake jolted awake to the sound of gun shots, and struggled to get his hand on his knife. After the pounding in his ears subsided, he realized that those bullets were not meant for him. The gang hadn't found him yet. *Guess those thugs found someone else. Poor bastards.* His heart thumped loudly in his ears and it was some time before he could relax again. *I guess it's true what they say, if you can hear the sound of the gunshots, then the bullet wasn't meant for you.*

CHAPTER 6

"Jiang-Li? Did you find anything?" Janey asked.

"No. I do not find anything yet." Jiang-Li, Janey, Francis and a few other support staff were the last remaining people in the sprawling office building. The inky, blackness of night was creeping its way from lab to office. The young women hadn't thought of an alternative light source until the most natural one of all decided to set in the west.

"Did you find anything, Janey?" Jiang-Li asked innocently.

"No. I didn't. Damn it!"

"Maybe we should ask Francis to help?" Janey glared at her in the twilight. Asking Francis for help was the last thing she wanted to do, now or ever. That man seem to revel in causing her nothing but anguish for no reason.

"No. He can find his own light." Janey's anger and contempt for her boss grew.

"What about a candle? Do we have any of this things?" Jiang-Li inquired.

"No. But I did think about lighting one of the burners in the lab for some light. Of course, the sparkers are electric." She leaned against the door of the conference room, dejected.

"So, no lighter then?"

"Nope."

"What about your bag?" Jiang-Li was pointing to the bag that Jake had packed for Janey. The two ladies had not even thought of it until now.

"Oh crap! I hope Jake packed us something good! I left it in the lab and it's pitch dark in there! Come on, let's go together." Carefully they crept along the darkened corridors, whispered voices could be heard from the cubical farm to their left.

"Almost there, I think." Janey was in the lead, her out stretched hand was feeling along the wall for orientation. The lab was just ahead on the right, but they had to maneuver across one intersection. She mentally kicked herself for her lapse. *Stupid. I should have kept that bag with me at all times! I hope to God that Jake put a lighter in there! I'm so sorry I got upset at you for buying all that crap. That's funny, calling it crap, when that crap might just save us from having to sit in the dark all night in a creepy laboratory.* Her fingers bounced along the smooth concrete wall until the cold metal door frame interrupted their course. Janey gasped in delight.

"I'm at the door now" she said, breaking the silence. She groped blindly for the handle until her hands found the familiar metal mechanism. She turned it and pushed it open. The door swung wide, but they couldn't tell the difference between the corridor and the lab interior.

"I left it on the counter near my workstation. Just a bit to the left now." Still gripping each other's hands tightly, they shuffled into the gaping maw that was their former lab. CRASH! The sound of the shattering glass was deafening in the dark.

"AAAHHhhh!" Janey was always prone to being startled. She hated it when Jake would jump out from a hiding place to make her jump and scream. He would laugh and laugh, sometimes with the kids watching and laughing too.

"Sorry." Jiang-Li said. "I think I just knocked over the beaker trays"

"Jeezus Jiang-Li! You almost gave me a heart attack!" They moved slowly and methodically with their hands stretched out in front of them, searching for a surface that was familiar. *I think my station is right.......here!* Her hand brushed a familiar piece of fabric. She grabbed it and turned it about, trying to figure out what it was. It was her lab coat! She remembered hanging it on her chair before they were instructed to go to the conference room earlier. *The bag should be on my chair.* Groping blindly she found nothing! *Oh no! Where did it go?*

"Jiang-Li, it's not here!"

"What? Why not?"

"I don't know, maybe Chris moved it." Janey was almost frantic now. In the panic and confusion she couldn't remember where it was placed.

"Looking for something?" A deep male voice, called out. It sounded strange. They froze.

"Who is that?" Janey practically screamed. *Shit, oh shit, oh shit! I can't see!* She was slowly spinning around in the darkness searching for a weapon to defend her and Jiang-Li.

"WHO'S HERE!" She shouted at the specter. The waves of sound bounced around the lab. Jake always said that she could make her voice echo even indoors. The soundwaves of her voice could reach a frequency that would reverberate in your ears, causing mild pain.

The darkness was suddenly driven back by a small flickering flame that appeared only a short distance away. Janey and Jiang-Li blinked as their eyes adjusted to the light source. They could see that it was one of those disposable Bic lighters. In the dim light they could see the light reflecting in the eyes of a now familiar face. The coldness in those eyes was clear.

"Francis! Goddamn it! Why didn't you tell us you were here! You scared the crap out of us! Where did you find the lighter?" Janey was peppering him with questions while trying to get her pulse rate to lower. He just stood there staring at them.

"Francis? Hello? Earth to Francis!" She waved her hand in front of his face. She could smell something burning. Something like meat, but not meat. She looked down at the lighter and realized the metal shroud was cooking his thumb! She snatched it out of his hand into her own. The light went out momentarily as she juggled it to keep from burning herself.

"Ow! " Francis was finally snapped out of his stupor. "What did you do that for?" She flicked the lighter to life and held it up.

"I did that because you weren't responding and you were cooking yourself! Dumbass."

"HEY! We might be stuck here after hours but I am still your boss! You are supposed to treat me with respect!" He stepped closer and she could make out the bag sitting open on the counter behind Francis. He must have opened it and was going through it when they walked in.

"Did you go through my bag?" She pointed to it.

"I didn't know who's it was. I thought it was fair game." He was caught and he knew it.

"Get away from me. Now!" Her eyes shot daggers at thim as he stepped back and moved closer to the doorway. She moved closer to the bag and saw that he had started taking things out. A ziploc bag of Clif Bars and powdered drink mix. A water filter and resevoir. A dark colored hoodie, tall socks and blue jeans along with a bra and panties were packed tightly into a gallon size ziploc. She spotted an older pair of sneakers that were still good, but out of style, sitting on the counter. She spied a small walkie-talkie with three AAA batteries rolling around inside in another ziploc bag. No flashlight. She felt around deeper inside the bag and came up empty. She was about to ask him if he found a flashlight when her hand bumped agains something hard. It wasn't in the main bag, but in an outside pouch pocket. She felt around with one hand, while trying to keep an eye on Francis. Her thumb was beginning to cook now, too. The pain was becoming almost unbearable, *I'm gonna have a blister for sure!* The dark, cold cylinder felt like salvation. She pulled it free and with a satisfying click, the bright light of 1300 lumens lit up the lab in a blaze of white light. It worked! Janey and Jiang-Li shielded their eyes from the sudden illumination. As their eyes became adjusted she realized that Francis was gone. *Great, now I gotta worry about Francis going off the deep end.*

"Jiang-Li, did you see where Francis went?"

"No, I did not. Sorry." She answered sheepishly.

"That's ok. Can you come over here and help me pack this stuff back up?"

"Yes, sure." Janey felt a sense of relief now that they had light. Light might mean safety and rescue!

================== * ==================

On the conference table was laid out the entire contents of the survival bag. In addition to the items that Francis had pulled out, was a green tarp with a reflective mylar coating on one side, an individual first aid kit or IFAK, a smaller survival kit, a folding lockblade knife, and another ziploc bag. Inside it was the true treasure.

"Oh Jake if you were here, I would kiss you!" Janey was ecstatic with joy at what she found.

"What are those?" Jiang-Li was leaning over Janey's shoulder but couldn't quite tell what was in the baggie.

"Candles!" Inside the bag were four extra tall votive style candles. She held up one long, white, tapered candle that had a thin wick at the top and a flared base at the bottom. Flicking the lighter back to life, she lit two of the candles. *Better to save a couple for later* she thought. She sat one on the table in front of herself then handed the other to Jiang-Li. She turned off the flashlight saving the battery power for later.

"I wish Chris was still here," lamented Jiang-Li.

"Yeah, me too." Chris had left a few hours before dark and was attempting to get home to her family.

They sat in silence for awhile, neither one wanting to interrupt the thoughts of the other. Janey thought of her husband, trekking from his office so many miles away. She was grateful that he had thought of her and she felt a bit of shame. Mostly at herself for not listening when he tried to get her to understand the possible dangers that could befall them and their family. She always said that she stores that information in his head. *No need to learn it when he already does! Right?* It was that kind of thinking that got her where she was now. *He is coming for me, and I need to be ready when he does.* Looking back down at the precious cargo, she took her change of clothes and the knife in one hand, and held the candle in the other.

"Jiang-Li, I'm gonna go change in the bathroom. I'll be right back, okay?"

"Okay" Jiang-Li responded, but didn't look at her. She was staring off into space, deep in thought. *Uh oh. Jiang-Li might be going on me too! Crap, crap, crappity crap!*

Moving through the building was much easier now, thanks to the candles. She had to move slow, but not as slow as before. She held her hand up by the flame, to keep the candle from going out. The corporate bathroom was just as elegant as she always knew it to be. *It is a germ ridden, bacteria filled dump! I hope Francis isn't hiding in the one of the stalls.* She slowly moved through

56

the restroom and opened each stall. Satisfied that the bathroom was empty and she was alone, she changed her clothes in peace.

"Jiang-Li, can you help me, again? I want to prop open the back door near the loading dock. Jake could be coming any time and I want to make sure that he can get in." Jiang-Li was right where Janey left her, in the conference room. She sat on the floor cross legged, staring out the windows.

"Jiang-Li?" No response. She was staring out the windows.

"Jiang-Li?" Again, no response. *Maybe louder.*

"JIANG-LI!" She jumped at the outburst, blinking back tears, she looked to Janey.

"I'm so sorry, Janey. What is it you wanted?" She slowly rose up, steadying herself on the table. Janey looked at her and wondered if maybe she should just go alone.

"I said, I want to prop open the outer doors near the loading dock in case Jake comes tonight."

"Oh. I can do that." She started walking in a daze toward the rear of the building. Janey stopped her from walking off into the pitch black with no light source.

"Jiang-Li, are you okay? Do you want to take a candle? Or maybe the flashlight?" She looked at Jiang-Li as if she was assessing one of her kids for injuries after a fall.

"Oh, yes please, the flashlight, if that is ok?" She finally met Janey's gaze and seemed to be back in control. Janey nodded and handed her the flashlight. She flipped it on and the bright beam of light leapt forth ahead of her as she briskly headed out the door and down the corridor.

"I think I need some fresh air," Jiang-Li said. She smiled and left Janey alone in the now cavernous and empty conference room. Janey stared down at the strewn contents of her bag. She didn't want Francis to come along while they were gone and steal anything. She quickly started scooping the different items and shoving them into the bag. The light from the flashlight was fading, Janey looked out doorway and called out to her friend.

"I'll meet you there!"

================== * ==================

Jiang-Li carefully walked through the empty building, past the cubical farm again. This time there was nothing but silence. Whoever was there before must have left or was possibly sleeping. The loading dock and materials processing area was in a vast mechanical open area attached to the back of the labs. Metal cages filled with solutions and acids and mixed chemicals in barrels were locked in with keyed padlocks. The lingering smell of lubricants and chemicals hung heavy in the air. The smallest sound was amplified in the cavernous room.

The rear entrance to the building was behind two electronically controlled doors separated by a small vestibule. Both locks needed a key card and electricity to unlock. A small double window with wire mesh was set in high up and to one side of the door. The small windows allowed one to look in or out and the wire was to prevent anyone from breaking in and turning the door handle. The window was at the perfect height for a fully grown man. Jiang-Li was not a grown man. She stood only five foot, one inch and was average for her family. The first door was no problem. She wedged it open with a random manual she had grabbed on her way there. The second and outer door was a heavy fire proof door. *What can I use here?* Jiang-Li was lost in thought. *Maybe I can find something outside, like a big rock!* She reached for the door handle.

"HELP ME!! LET ME IN! HELP ME PLEASE!" A woman's voice cried from outside. The frantic voice grew louder as she approached the door. The stranger hammered on the door, it was a fast, deep and pulsing rhythm.

Jiang-Li yelped at the sound. *How did she know I was here? The FLASHLIGHT!* She quickly turned off light, the scared persons only beacon of hope, drowning herself in the darkness.

"NOOOO!!! Please help me! I won't tell them, I swear! Ahhhh! Keep away!" The woman's voice faded and the pounding stopped. *She must be running away,* Jiang-Li thought. Quietly she raised herself up and onto her tiptoes. She could barely see out the window. There seemed to be a couple of fires on sticks coming near. *Torches?* Through the cracks in the door jam, she could hear several voices.

"There she is!"

"Get her!"

"That bitch bit me, she's gonna get it now!" Jiang-Li gasped and dropped back down. The group was searching the parking lot. The frightened woman screamed again.

"Please no! I'm sorry, I'm so sorry! Please let me go! I won't tell anyone!"

"That's right bitch, you won't tell anyone, cause you'll be dead!" KABLAM, KABLAM! The screaming ceased. The only sound was muffled laughter. Jiang-Li couldn't believe what she just heard. *Some poor woman was asking for help and I didn't help her. She might be shot, or worse, dead.* Jiang-Li silently made her way back into the main part of the building, back to Janey in the conference room. She saw that Francis was there too, neither one was talking.

"Jiang-Li, are you ok? I heard some loud noises and thought it might be gunshots." Francis was speaking to her, and he sounded concerned but the look behind his eyes told a different story. He didn't care. He didn't care about them at all. She turned to Janey and told her about the encounter. They slowly made their way through the rooms until they arrived at an outside wall with windows that faced the back parking lot.

In the moonlight they saw a group of people surrounding something or someone on the ground. They could hear muffled voices but couldn't make out what was being said. The thing on the ground was moving, almost like writhing. The moving torch light was making it hard to figure out what they were standing over.

"Is that guy pointing a gun?" Francis pointed to one of the group members, just as a flash and deafening boom shook the window. KABLAM! The form on the ground stopped moving. The group now satisfied, crossed through the parking lot, never glancing back. They headed toward the neighboring building, a five story hotel for business travellers. One person hung back and looked down at the form on the ground. They saw him crouch down and rifle through the dead person's pockets.

"Who is that out there?" Francis wondered aloud.

"I don't know" Janey answered. "Jake, Where are you?"

DAY 2

CHAPTER 7

The sounds of morning stirred Jake from his slumber. The sweet song of robins and starlings chirped in the trees above him piercing the air. *Great, the birds are just as bad here as they are at home!* He glanced at his watch and could barely see that it was almost 6 a.m. The encounter from the previous night still loomed over his thoughts. His back and legs ached from tossing and turning on the cold, hard ground. He could feel his calf and foot muscles still burning from the previous days trek.

He shifted around in his "bed", carefully running through the days plans when he remembered the gang that was looking for him last night. He stopped moving, highly aware that his position could be given away. His senses were instantly on high alert. The birds continued chirping above in the trees and a few squirrels skittered about on the ground. Nature seemed relaxed and unafraid. *I don't hear anyone or see anyone, that could be good or bad. If I can't see them, they can't see me.* He decided to get up and get moving, but slowly, and quietly!

Knowing that the tarp isn't exactly like a silk sheet, he moved slowly and as quiet as a field mouse. *I don't want my location broadcast for all to hear.* After he had stowed his tarp he pulled out his small, field binoculars. *Thank you God! So glad I packed these.* He had hoped that he wouldn't need them, but he was very grateful to have them now! He scanned the area around his hiding place, and didn't see anyone. Slowly and as carefully as he could, he extracted himself from the shelter of his position.

Once clear from the brambles and thorns, Jake dropped back to one knee and scanned again. Now free from the bushes, which obstructed much of his view, he confirmed to himself that no one was around. *Huh, gang must have gone home.*

His abdomen suddenly roiled and gurgled. The sound of his stomach was almost loud enough to hear on the outside! With the power knocked out and the vehicular traffic sounds gone he had noticed that the sounds of nature were much louder now! No traffic noise, or people talking, or planes flying overhead. *Weird. Oh well. Gotta change my socks and have a bite to eat.* It was one of the rules he taught his scouts, keep your feet dry and they will thank you for it! Hydration was a very close second. Hydrated scouts were happy scouts and dehydrated scouts were dead scouts. He dug through his pack, and changed his socks, taking a spare second to tie his pair from the previous day to the outside of his pack to dry in the open air.

A chocolate chip Clif Bar and a bottle of water later and he was ready to go. *Not exactly the breakfast of champions but I'll take it.* He pulled out his printed maps, and checked his watch. He figured on about eight more miles to go. By his pace from yesterday it should take him about three hours to get to Janey's workplace. *Not too bad, I can do this.* He carefully shouldered the pack and looked to the main road. The large red barn stood between him and the roadway. *Hmm. I don't remember a barn from last night.*

He looked at the large and imposing structure and wondered how he hadn't seen it the previous night. Behind it sat a sprawling playscape typical of city parks. The slides and multicolored monkey bars were all suspended above a thick bed of wood chips to pad the inevitable falls. *Hope for the best, plan for the worst,* he though as he patted his trusty lockblade, carefully stored in his front pocket.

Walking and hiking were two very different activities. One required no gear, just you and your shoes. The other required thought and preparation. The correct footwear and right size pack made all the difference. Then, of course, the gear that was packed inside and how it was packed was just as important. Jake was glad he had packed the items he did. He had faith that those precious items would help get him home. While he was deep in thought, Jake carelessly stepped out into the playscape area and was startled by a familiar voice.

"Hey man! Nice pack!" In his early morning stupor and thoughts of hiking versus walking, Jake failed to notice the three youths sitting atop one of the slides. One of them yelled out to him.

"I said, nice pack!" He was dressed in jeans, hung low, a black leather jacket and a red bandana wrapped tightly around his head. Jake noticed that all three had the same red bandana. *It's that gang, Goddammit,* he thought. Caught, Jake turned and saw them climbing down out of the playscape and advancing towards him. A flash of bright yellow caught his eye. One of the thugs was wearing bright neon yellow sneakers. *Yep, same stupid yellow sneakers.* He gripped his hiking stick tightly in one hand and slowly slid his thumb and forefinger of his other hand into his pocket and prepared to pull the knife free, if needed.

Jake slowed his pace, but didn't stop. He scanned the area for the rest of their friends, but saw no one else.

"Good Morning!" he said with a nod while turning and continuing toward the street and freedom.

"Hey man, hold up! We just want to talk!" Sneakers yelled.

"Yeah, just talk! Ha haha!" His friend said, his voice dripping with malice. Jake didn't want to "hold up" knowing that his pack and its contents was the "toll" for their "bridge".

"Shut up, Junior! You wanna scare him off?" said Sneakers

"Hey man, he ain't stopping, what are we gonna do?" Jake pumped his legs harder, walking faster. He saw that the path to the main road led past the barn. *Oh shit, oh shit, I don't want to fight! Why won't they leave me alone! Surival of the fittest. It's either me or them and it ain't about to be me.* With a new found resolve he looked at the barn and a plan started to form.

"Get him!" Sneakers yelled and their footfalls changed from walking to full out running. Jake heard this new command and sprinted for the barn. As he rounded the corner of the barn, he unclipped the pack and tossed it aside. He dropped the stick to the ground and with a quick flick of his wrist, the knife was out, opened and locked. He turned to get in position as one of the thugs came flying around the corner. The knife flashed quickly, almost like it was guided by another's hand. The thug was lifted off his feet by the blow and driven to the ground, the knife planted deep in his chest. The thugs eyes went wide as he screamed in pain and started coughing blood. Jake wrenched the knife free, causing a spurt of blood to shoot from the young man's chest. Nice Pack and Sneakers had come around the corner and witnessed what Jake had done. They dug their heels in and tried to stop from experiencing the same fate. Gravity and inertia, however, had something else in mind for these two. They both tumbled to the ground as they tried to get a safe distance away from the knife wielding madman.

Nice Pack was first to his feet and he quickly lifted his dirty t-shirt to show that he had a handgun tucked in his waistband. A cowardly show of bravado that was lost on Jake. His fight or flight response was in high gear for fighting.

"Don't son. You don't want this to happen to you, do you?" Jake asked him as he pointed to the now still form, bleeding on the ground. The young man's eyes darted back and forth from his friend to his friends' killer. The knife, blade now coated in bright red blood, was gripped tightly in Jake's hand. It felt like it was almost vibrating.

"I don't want to hurt you! I didn't want to hurt him! Please, leave me alone!" Jake was pleading with him to back down.

"Junior! Get that motherfucker!" Sneakers growled out the command to his crony. He had regained his footing and still thought that he could win this. *Nice Pack had a name!* Junior, ever the good foot soldier, obeyed his leader and went for the handgun still tucked in his waistband. Jake lunged forward and punched him twice in the face while still holding the knife. The punches exploded Junior's nose and he screamed out in pain and anger. He rushed forward and reached out for Jake, but Jake had retreated and was preparing for the retaliation he knew was coming. He stepped forward and stabbed the knife under Junior's chin. He angled the blade up, effectively clamping the thugs mouth shut. He pushed hard, driving it deep into the young man's skull. Blood poured forth over Jake's hands as he yanked the knife free. Junior's eyes rolled back in his head as his body dropped to the ground.

"NOOOO!!" Yellow Sneakers bellowed and tackled Jake. They struggled for control of the knife, which seemed odd to Jake since he could see that Sneakers had a gun in his waistband too. Jake threw him off and both were on their feet in seconds.

Sneakers was filled with blind rage at this man who had just killed two of his friends. He wanted to see Jake's head on a pike and his guts fed to his two pitbulls waiting at home. He lunged at Jake again, but this time Jake was ready for it. He accepted the tackle and instead of trying to keep the knife from being taken, he deftly folded it closed and let if fall to the ground. Sneakers had the upper hand and started beating on Jake. Fists flew wildly, pummeling his chest, arms and head. Clearly this young man had never boxed or been in a real fist fight, as his blows were light and ineffectual. Jake laid on the ground, blocking and deflecting the blows while he waited for his opening. He reached for the gun in Sneaker's waistband.

The flurry of fists was starting to slow and Jake siezed this moment to act. He reached out and grabbed the gun and smashed the butt of it against the head of his would-be murderer. Sneakers screamed out and fell off of Jake, gripping his now bleeding head.

"What the fuck, man? We just wanted to talk!" He spat at Jake, realizing the fight was lost.

"Yeah, right. Talk? What about, that's a nice pack, we should take it? Or get him? That doesn't sound so nice to me!" Jake's anger was really ramped up now. The adrenaline was coursing through his veins, pumping him up for more violence.

"I'm gonna fuck you up, sucka!" Sneakers was still in fight mode too. *Should I just take this asshole out and not worry about it?* The coldness of the thought, scared him deeply. *No, I can't do that. Although....* The adrenaline was fading and rational thought was starting to take control.

"Now what am I going to do with you?" Jake looked down at the thug just as Sneakers dove for his legs. Jake was ready for this attack. Jake swung the gun again, and this time the butt of the gun found it's mark and Sneakers went down hard. His body lay still on the ground.

Jake knelt down and checked for a pulse. Satisfied that the hoodlum was only unconscious and not dead, Jake collapsed down next to the young man. Breathing heavily and feeling the familiar tightness in his lungs that signaled a need for a hit off of his inhaler, he looked around for his pack and stick. They sat near the barn, a few feet from the first body. He looked down at his trembling hands, coated in sticky red blood and his heart pumped harder. The fight or flight response was finally wearing off. He looked at the carnage about him and shook his head. He took a few deep breaths to try and calm his nerves, but it only served to slow the tremors. *It was me or them, me or them. What am I gonna do now?* He took another steadying breath.

"Well, shit!"

CHAPTER 8

As the morning sun began it's climb heavenward, shining it's light and warmth upon the world, the darkened office felt more like a tomb. The cubicles were spread out in the vast open office floor. Janey and Jiang-Li had taken the cubes farthest from Francis's office to try and distance themselves from him. Jiang-Li had seen him pacing in the hallway.

Sometime after midnight Jiang-Li was awoken by the sound of voices. She carefully rose to investigate and found Francis talking to himself. She rushed back and woke Janey, telling her what she just witnessed. They agreed to relocate to a different cube. Francis had watched them pick out their cube earlier, but now they wanted to make sure that he wouldn't easily find them. They settled on one along an interior wall and away from any intersections. It was also away from the windows. Which was good, since they didn't want to be seen from outside either.

The sun continued it's unabated climb until its light finally shone through the tinted windows. The cube farm was becoming illuminated enough to rouse

Janey from a fitful night of sleep. She had had a dream that Jake wasn't able to get to her. Something had happened to him and she was now alone. It had felt so real, that when she did awake, her heart was thudding loudly in her chest and pulsing in ears. It was so loud in her head that for a split second she thought she had gone deaf!

Janey stretched and looked for Jiang-Li. She was gone. Again, her heart started racing!

"Jiang-Li?" she whispered, not wanting to be heard too far away. "Jiang-Li? Where are you?" This time a little bit louder.

"Over here." Jiang-Li answered. Relieved, Janey stood up and her back immediately spasmed. She took a deep breath and focused inward, forcing her shoulders and back to relax. She was so tense, that her back threatened to seize up. Janey had suffered from back pains and muscle aches for years and sleeping on the hard floor of the office did not do her any favors. She continued stretching as she made her way to Jiang-Li.

"Good morning Jiang-Li! How long have you been up?" She said softly. Since last night they didn't really know who was still in the building and of those that they did know about, they knew one wasn't doing so well mentally.

"I didn't sleep." Jiang-Li said as she continued to gaze out the windows. The north parking lot was full of cars and trucks, that would never be driven again. It was an eerie site but Jiang-Li never wavered. It struck Janey as just a bit peculiar. She carefully moved closer to Jiang-Li and the window, trying to see what Jiang-Li was looking at.

"Why not? Was the floor too hard?" Janey continued scanning the lot until she saw them. A pair of bare feet, sticking out from behind a shiny new sports car. The body was at such an angle they couldn't see the person's face. But they thought they recognized the khaki pants and the garishly purple polo. Near to him was another body, a female form.

"Are those the people from last night?" Janey asked cautiously. Jiang-Li stood mute, then nodded slowly. They stood there for a time, staring at the horror, the tragedy of last night.

"Is that Bill Shannon?" Janey asked quietly.

"WHAT IN THE FUDGE!" A deep voice roared behind them.

"AAAhhh!" Jiang-Li had collapsed into a heap. The bellowing sound of Francis's voice startled them from their thoughts. Janey's heart started a third race. *Dammit! He found us,* she thought. She furrowed her brow in anger as her lips curled in disgust. Francis was standing over them, eyes bulging and chest heaving in obvious anger.

"JESUS CHRIST, Francis! How long have you been standing there?" She asked, but was terrified of the answer. Jiang-Li sat upon the floor, still weeping. Janey knelt down and comforted her.

"Just a minute or two." He answered calmly, his demeanor had changed in an instant. He was now transfixed on the two bodies outside the building. He had gone from raging lunatic to calm psychopath instantly. The sudden shift in his attitude struck Janey as odd and dangerous.

"It's okay, Jiang-Li. Shhh. Calm down. It was just Francis." She glared at him as she spat his name. He glanced at the floor sheepishly, but didn't apologize. Jiang-Li had regained her composure enough to answer him.

"Yes, that is Bill Shannon, but I do not know the other woman. They were outside last night and I saw them get attacked by a group of people. I could have let them in the building. I could have saved them. But I did nothing!" She buried her face in her hands and started crying again, this time in shame for her inaction to save those people.

"It's not your fault Jiang-Li. If you had let Bill and that other lady in then the gang might have tried to get in here too! You saved us, Jiang-Li!" Janey was trying to get her to see the positive side. *What little there was of it.* Janey looked out the window and then to

Francis. He returned her stare until he couldn't take it anymore and glanced away. Suddenly the nap of the carpeting became very interesting to him. He was not going to help. *If she saw a gang kill those two people, where did they go? They could still be out there. Will my heart ever stop racing!*

"Jiang-Li, where did the gang go?" she asked gently. Jiang-Li looked out the window and pointed to the hotel on the far side of the lot. *Great. Just freaking great. There could be a gang waiting to kill us if we leave, or kill Jake when he gets here! What in the hell are we going to do now?* Jiang-Li quickly stood up and started wailing.

"I could have helped more! I should have done something! I AM A BAD PERSON, I SHOULDN'T BE HERE!" Jiang-Li struggled hysterically and broke from Janey's embrace. She bolted past Francis and ran for the loading dock. They raced after her, each trying to get ahead of the other. The outer door was in sight and they feared the worst if she was able to breach it. Francis reached her first. He spun her around and starting shaking her.

"JIANG-LI, SNAP OUT OF IT! KNOCK IT OFF, JIANG-LI!" She thrashed in his arms, like a 125lb marlin, trying to break free from a fisherman's line but he was too strong for her.

"JIANG-LI, STOP!" He slapped her across the face, once, twice, three times in rapid succession. Janey watched on in horror as he assaulted her friend and colleauge. His face was devoid of emotion and Janey thought that he looked like a robot.

"FRANCIS! WHAT ARE YOU DOING?" She screamed. He couldn't hear her over Jiang-Li's wailing. Janey launched herself at him, flailing and smacking at his arms and back. He turned and pushed her away, her feet flew out from under her as she tripped on the uneven floor and tumbled to the ground. She scrambled to her feet and looked around the loading dock area, trying to find something to use to save Jiang-Li from this lunatic. She spotted the "White Elephant" table. It was a small table of miscellaneous objects and lab supplies that was no longer needed but was free to a good home. On the table sat a big, red, Swingline stapler. Someone must have set it there by mistake or maybe it was providence!

She snatched the stapler and swung the hinged end towards Francis's face. It smashed him square in the nose, and caused a sudden cascade of blood to flow forth down his face. He released his grip on Jiang-Li as the force of the blow launched him backwards. He tumbled to the ground and cupped his damaged nose. He winced and cried out.

"AGHGH!! MY NOSE! YOU BROKE MY NOSE!" *He's more concerned about his nose, than what he was just doing to one of his employees!* Janey was shaking. She didn't know if it was from fear or anger. She was terrified of what he might do next. Looking at Jiang-Li, she was rewarded with the answer. She sat on the ground, red handprints showing visibly on her cheeks still wet with tears. This poor woman who was suffering over a trauma that only she could know, had been traumatized again by a man who took pleasure in seeing people in agony. It was not fear Janey felt, it was raw, pure, unadulterated rage. She looked down at the stapler and it felt white hot in her hand. She wasn't done with it yet. She stood up and positioned herself between Francis and Jiang-Li.

"GOOD! I HOPE I DID, YOU SICK ASSHOLE!" She spat at him. He staggered to his feet and his eyes darted back and forth between the two women. Janey stepped between her friend and boss.

"If you even think about touching her or me again, I won't just break your nose. I just might do something worse." She spoke with measured anger and pain, hoping that he would get the idea and back down. He was pinching his nostrils trying to stem the flow of blood but he was failing horribly.

"You are in SO much trouble now! This little incident is going in your personnel file and it just might get you fired! What about that? Huh! Yeah, your ass is grass now, little miss do-no-wrong! You have really stepped in it now!" His voice sounded pinched and whiney. Janey was amazed at what he was saying! *Is he actually trying to threaten me with being fired. Now? It's the end of the world as we knew it and he is going to fire me?*

"No. I don't think so. You see, Francis, I am not going to let you fire me today. You aren't going to fire Jiang-Li either. In fact, you are going back to your office and I don't EVER want to see you again!" Francis swore her eyes glowed red. His anger quickly to fear. He stammered a reply.

"Why don't you just..." She cut him off sharply.

"WHY DON'T YOU JUST SHUT THE HELL UP AND GET OUT!" Janey bellowed. Jake was fond of saying that her voice could reach a certain frequency that would make his ears pulse. She did that now and with such force that for a moment Francis let go of his nose and covered his ears. Her voice echoed in the loading dock. They stood staring at each other for a second. Who would blink first. Janey had had enough and stepped forward. Francis flinched at her sudden movement and scrambled for the doorway to the offices, making a safe retreat.

Jiang-Li and Janey looked at each other, the adrenaline still flowing, until the absurdity of the confrontation overwhelmed them. They burst out laughing.

"Goddamn! That felt GOOD!" Janey said.

"Thank you for rescuing me. You didn't have to." Janey looked at her and smiled. She set the stapler back on the table and wrapped Jiang-Li up in a warm embrace. They laughed and cried and finally laughed again. Jiang-Li stepped back, wiped her nose on her sleeve and rubbed her cheeks.

"I am hungry. Do you think there is food somewhere here?" Jiang-Li asked while wiping the last of her tears.

"I think so. Let's go check our new "Lunch Room!" The corporate think tank had decided that it would be more cost efficient to change out the vending machines that contained unhealthy choices with a new "Market" style eating area. The room was largely unchanged except that where the familiar vending machines once stood all filled with artery clogging deliciousness, now held three large refrigerators with glass fronts. The new healthy and organic items sat in the dark coolers slowly warming.

Together they checked each fridge for something that was edible. After checking the last fridge for food, they both agreed that there was nothing that they wanted or should eat. The coolers had been down since yesterday and Janey was one to throw away food that had gotten warm for fear of bacteria or contamination. *Food poisoning is nothing to laugh at*, she thought. Together they stared at the shelves of snack foods. Cheese crackers, and chips, energy bars and cough drops, licorice and bags of artificially flavored fruit candies. *Well, there goes my diet,* Janey thought. She grabbed a bag of potato chips and turned to Jiang-Li. "Bon Appetit!"

CHAPTER 9

The early morning dew had saturated the grass and low bushes. In his haste to outrun his pursuers, Jake had tossed his pack into an unmowed grassy area and it too was now saturated. He dug out a length of paracord and cut an arms length off of one end. He grimaced inwardly as he heard his friend Matts' voice echo in his head. *The worst thing you can do to a rope is cut it!*

"Sorry buddy, gotta do it." He mumbled.

Matt was one of Jake's most trusted and knowledgeable friends. They had met six years ago at a cub scout meeting. Their son's were in different dens and ages, but they were both on the pack committee and had hit it off right away. Some might say that they were kindred spirits. They had each other's back, all the time. Matt was an Eagle scout and was Jake's right hand man at the Troop meetings. Being a Scoutmaster had some perks, learning about knots was one! Matt was fond of teaching Jake a few new ones every year at summer camp.

Jake rolled the still unconscious leader of the gang, whom he had named Sneakers, on to his belly. He pulled the hoodlum's hands behind his back and secured them with expertly tied knots, wrapping them tightly. Next he tied his feet together at the ankles, then secured the hands and feet to each other. Jake stood up and admired his work. He had tied up the thug like a hog in a rodeo. *He's not going anywhere anytime soon!* Satisfied that even if the guy woke up, he would be in no position to move, Jake searched him for anything of value. He found a nice, black handled lock-blade knife similar to the one that he already had in his pocket and a few extra magazines for the handgun, a pack of cigarettes, a Bic lighter, and a baggie of unknown "herbs and spices". Jake took it all and packed it away.

Searching the other two bodies he came away with much of the same. He had gained two additional handguns with extra magazines. He turned them over in his hands, making sure that the safety was engaged. Jake had gone shooting with his brother-in-law a few times so he was somewhat familiar with handguns. Not all were the same, but they were alike enough that he could make sure they were safe. He knew that some handguns didn't even have a safety mechanism. Thankfully, these did.

It appeared that this was a gang of druggies and deliquents. *At least I have some more protection than a knife now. I will have to teach Janey how to use one of these when I get to her.*

They paused as he looked over the bodies, taking in the damage he had wrought. He saw two young men, who would not go home because of his actions. *But it was me or them! They were out trying to get some thrills or to make some money. Money that was now practically useless!.*

The blood was sticky and the air smelled of metal. Their shirts were covered in it. Jake had hunted in his youth, and had done his fair share of field dressing game, so he was not unaccustomed to the sight and smell of blood. But this seemed different. It wasn't because it was human blood, he had seen a lot of that as well. He was very accident prone as a child which required many trips to the ER for stitches. From head wounds to puncture wounds he had seen more before twelve years old than most kids. All together that was a lot of blood and a lot of physical pain.

This was different because he was the reason for it. He was the cause for it to flow out onto the ground from the bodies of the two young men. Two young men who had mothers and fathers, that loved them. Two young men that had made a bad decision some time in their lives to join a gang. His hands started to shake again and his breathing quickened. *My GOD what have I done!* Tears started to stream down his face. He buried his face in his blood soaked hands. He sat and wept

================= * =================

Jake thought that he should do something with the bodies. Something respectful. He didn't know if they were religious young men or not. He himself wasn't THAT religious but being raised in the Catholic faith, he made the sign of the cross over them. He said the Lord's Prayer and a silent prayer of forgiveness. After he was done, he dragged the bodies into the bushes behind the barn, leaving a long trail of blood in the dirt and grass. *I hope it rains soon, it will help with the cleansing,* he thought. He found a nice spot in a small clearing and stopped. He gently placed their hands on their stomachs and closed their eyes. Once again, he said the Lord's Prayer and walked back to the front of the barn.

"Hey man, untie me!" *Great he's up.* Jake had hoped to be long gone when Sneaker's awoke.

"What the fuck, man! Let me go! I will fuck you up!" He struggled harder, not knowing that the scout knots Jake had tied only get tighter and tighter the more you pulled. He wanted to get back on the road and didn't really have time for this.

"You don't know who you dealin with! Once I get out of here, and get my brotha's, we gonna plant yo white ass in the ground!" Jake turned to face the thug, waiting patiently for him to calm down, but that didn't seem likely. He squatted down low so they could see eye to eye. He lashed out and back handed the thug across the mouth. The blow was much harder than Jake had intended and the thug was knocked clear over onto his side, his yellow sneakers flashed in the sunlight. Before he started ranting again, Jake took the opportunity to speak his mind. He voice was low as he growled.

"Listen to me, I didn't want to do this. I take no pleasure in what I have done. I tell you now that I will take this with me to the grave. I just want to get home to my wife and kids. I did not want to do it, but you and your friends forced me to. Do you understand?"

"FUCK YOU!" he spat at Jake. He realized that this was going no where. Jake stood up and brushed the dirt from his hands.

"We can do this one of three ways. Option One. I can untie you and we leave peacefully in opposite directions. Let bygones be bygones. Forget this ever happened and chalk it up to a bad set of circumstances and decisions."

"KISS MY ASS, CRACKER!"

"Option Two. I can leave you here, tied up, but add the extra fun of some Duct tape across your mouth. Then I drag your ass into the bushes and you can hope that your friends find you, and untie you. By then I'll be long gone and a distant memory." He glared at Jake as sweat trickled down his face.

"Yeah, you leave me alive and I will track you down and put you down. Then I will find yo wife and kids and do what I want, when I want, to 'em." He was trying to goad Jake into fighting him, but it was not working. Jake stared at him, and took a deep breath. He let it out slowly as he pulled the handgun from his own waist band. He pulled the slide back to see if there was a bullet in the chamber. Satisfed that it was loaded, he looked back at Sneakers.

"Option Three. I put your sorry ass down now and never think of you or your friends again. I have all of your weapons, and your friends' too. There is nothing here for me. I wanted to leave here peacefully. I don't want it to go this way. Now you choose." Seeing the gun out and loaded had filled Sneakers with bravado, not fear as Jake had hoped it would.

"Go on, muthafucka, do it! You cap me and you ain't no betta than us!" Jake circled behind Sneakers, the gun firmly in his grasp.

"You let me live, and I will get you, AND yo family!" His head whipped from side to side as he tried to see whre Jake had gone.

Jake had stopped behind Sneakers and raised the gun. *He was right. I do this and I am no better than him. Damn it.* Changing his grip on the handgun, Jake stepped forward and swung it hard. The butt of the gun connected squarely with the side of Sneakers head. Once again he was pushed into unconciousness. *Dear God, I hope I did the right thing,* Jake thought.

He dug the roll of Duct tape out of the pack, and set about taping Sneaker's mouth shut. He quickly wrapped the still bound hands and legs tightly. Once he was done he scanned the area for a hiding place. Jake decided to drag Sneaker's body deep into the bushes near the barn. *He should be hidden from view for quite some time. I hope I never see him again, but if I do, now I am a bit more ready. I hope I made the right choice. Time to go.*

CHAPTER 10

Even for vending machine food, it was food and they were happy for it. Janey and Jiang-Li spent the rest of the morning in the market room, eating by the light that filtered in through the skylight. They talked of their families and of what they were going to do now that the power was out and may never come back.

"Ya know, I always thought my husband was wasting his time with reading about survival stuff! I am SO glad he did!" Janey said, in between bites from her King-Size Snickers bar.

"You said he was a scout? I thought that the boys are scouts. Isn't he a little bit old to be a scout?" Jiang-Li asked.

"Well, he is a scout leader. My son, Joey, is a scout. Jake was never a scout. His younger brothers were in cub scouts." Jiang-Li looked confused.

"Cub scouts is for younger boys six to eleven years old. Boy scouts is for eleven to eighteen year olds. Jake went along with his brothers as a sort of chaperone or helper. When Joey was born, Jake talked of the day when he could get him enrolled in scouting. I guess I never really thought about how much it meant to him." Janey trailed off, thoughts of her husband and son filled her mind.

"Means to him." She corrected herself. *Past tense, I spoke about him in the past tense! NO! He is coming for me and he should be here today.*

"WHAT ARE YOU DOING! That is company property you are stealing!" Francis had found them. He stood in the doorway, mouth agape and eyes wide at what he was seeing. Two of his, soon-to-be former, employees were eating the food that was bought and paid for by the company! *This was downright theft of the highest order! How dare they,* he thought.

"I will not stand for this! Put it all back!" He glared at them like some irate parent who had walked in on the children playing in flour. *Classic Francis.* Janey returned his glare, with interest.

"No." said Jiang-Li.

"Excuse me?" he answered astonishingly. She had never stood up to Francis, or anyone for that matter! Jiang-Li stood up and squared her shoulders. She looked to Janey for support and strength.

"I said, NO! We are hungry and this food is here for us to use. If you don't like it then you can....what is it called?" She looked at Janey, then suddenly remembered, "bill me!"

"Bill you?!? Bill you?!!? Now you listen here, you little-"

"Don't you say it." Janey growled. She had risen to her feet quietly and like a leopard her muscles were tense and ready to strike. He turned his head to see her now up and ready to defend herself and Jiang-Li.

"Say, what? I wasn't going to say anything," he sneered.

"You leave us alone and we will leave you alone. Just go back to your office and when my husband gets here we will be gone."

"And what if I don't go back to my office, then what?" His confidence had returned and he was getting aggressive again.

"You better hope that Jake doesn't see you when he gets here.

"Is that a threat? Are you threatening me? You are already on thin ice as it is. I don't think you have any idea what the consequences of your past and current actions are going to have!"

"Yes, it damn well IS a threat! No Francis, YOU have no idea how much pain and misery you have put me and my family through. The late nights, and missed events. The bickering over non-existent raises, and sleepless nights worrying about this hell-hole!" She was moving forward with every verbal blow.

"That's not my fault!" Francis finally realized that she was within striking distance, and he instinctively reached for his now bandaged nose.

"Oh yes it is! My husband has as much hatred, if not more, for you than I do! With the state of the world now, how safe does that make you feel? Hm? Well?" He was backing away from her with each step she took closer. His eyes darted around the room, looking for something to defend himself with but found nothing.

"I go home every night worried that I missed a sample or forgot to turn off the ICP machine. I am tired, worn out, beaten down and it's all. Because. Of. YOU! I do hope you are here when Jake comes for me. I hope you start some shit, because he has said that he would love to beat the living CRAP out of you!"

"Do you even think he could get this far? He would have to be in peak physical condition to even try!" Again, more bravado but little substance.

"Yes I do. He will get here and rescue me. Then he will get us to our kids and then get us all home!"

"How do you even know what he is capable of?" He sneered at her.

"You don't get it. He is a trained Scoutmaster in charge of thirty young men. Young men that he trains in knots, outdoor living, fire starting, and knife safety. He has taken scouts on Wilderness Survival training! Young men that he takes on multiple mile backpack hikes so I know he can hike this far! He camps in the outdoors, sometimes with no tent or shelter! He eats dehydrated food and has all of the equipment to do it. He IS coming for me, of that I have no doubt."

Francis had been backing up slowly as Janey advanced with every fact. She also had been getting louder and louder.

"I know my husband will come for me, because he loves me, and he wants me to be safe. I know my husband also hates you, so leave us ALONE!" She shouted this last word at him. Francis, finally spooked, bolted from the room. Jiang-Li stared at her, slack jawed. Janey looked back at her and shrugged her shoulders.

"What?"

CHAPTER 11

Jake walked along what was once a major traffic artery for the metro Detroit area but was now a glorified parking lot. The clicking of his hiking stick hitting the asphalt echoed off the cars. The image before him was surreal. Thousands of vehicles, from cars and trucks, to motorcycles and panel vans sat unmoving in the concrete like river. The amount of circuitry that was needed to make them work, was ironically the same thing that was stopping them from operating. *What I would give for a early 80's or even 70's car right about now! Hell, even a bicycle would do!* He thought of the older model vehicles with little to no computers. *Surely they must have been spared damage from the EMP pulse.*

He walked briskly, trying to put some distance between Sneakers and himself. The further away from the park and the remains of the morning, the better. The incident was still fresh in his mind. The adrenaline had worn off and the shaking from shock had begun. At first he thought he was cold, but that wasn't it, mostly because he was sweating and it was already getting quite warm out. He finally figured out that every time he thought of those two men he killed, he shook. He would have to stop and close his eyes, then breathe deeply and tell himself, *it was either me or them, me or them. I have to survive.* He focused on images of Janey and his kids in his minds eye to give him the resolve he needed to soldier on.

Strange, I haven't heard any noises from the neighborhoods. He stole a look at his watch and saw that it was only 8:15am. *Only eight fifteen!?!?* He was surprised at the time since so much had happened already today. It was still early, but there should be some people up. He could hear the distant rumble of an engine, possibly a generator. The bubbly sounds of children playing floated on the air to him as he walked. But none of those sounds were close by. It was then that he took noticed of the open grassy meadow behind a tall ornate wrought iron fence. The only structures he could make out were small stone plinths and slabs. A cemetery.

He knew the name of it immediately, Roseland Park Cemetery. His wife's grandparents and aunt were buried there. Many years ago, he had taken her, the kids and his father-in-law there to pay respects. Jake was a amateur genealogist as a hobby. *Hobby is putting it mildly, I get obsessed with things.* It was an obsession that led him to that cemetery, and it was his newest obsession that was helping to keep him alive.

The sun climbed inevitably higher and higher in the sky while warming the earth below. It was this warmth that was finally getting to Jake.

"I need a break!" he wheezed. Seeing the gate up ahead, he bee-lined to the entrance and went in. Besides being a nice open park-like place, it was full of dead folks. *Hopefully that will keep the riff-raff out!* Most people avoid cemeteries for various reasons, all of which were lost on Jake.

A huge stone mausoleum stood a short distance down the main drive. It was designed to hold the remains and cremains of loved ones that could not afford a ground burial. On the eastern wall of the structure was a large mural depicting Jesus healing the sick and comforting the wounded. Behind the Lord, a chorus of angels welcomed the dead into the gates of heaven. *There's gonna be line up there now!*

The sick and diseased would soon be the dead and dying if power wasn't restored soon. Jake knew the potential for death after a power outage was high if it wasn't restored in a week.

If you were on a ventilator, needed kidney dialysis or dependent on daily doses of insulin, you were on the short list to get in to heaven. No power meant, no ventilator, no dialysis, and no refrigeration for insulin. *I wonder if the EMP affected the airlines too? How many poor*

unfortunate souls fell to their deaths from the skies above?
The thought was sobering to say the least.

Shaking the macabre thoughts from his mind, he placed his stick against the wall and unshouldered his pack. He sat down with his back to the wall in a nice shaded spot. 12 Mile road was behind him and the other major thoroughfare, Woodward Avenue was only about a hundred yards away. *Hopefully I am hidden enough.* He dug out his rescue inhaler and took two puffs. *I'll just rest here for a few minutes until I catch my breath.*

While enjoying the morning air and sun, he checked his map and figured that he was only about four miles away from the scene of the incident. A waft of cold morning air washed over him. The hair on his neck stood up and the birds ceased their morning calls. Jake sat up straight, his head spun about like on a swivel. He felt like he was being watched. Startled, he jumped to his feet and shouldered his pack and grabbed his hiking stick. He scanned the surrounding area, but saw no one. *No, I'm not being watched, but I feel like I'm being judged. Who would be here to judge me?* Looking up, he saw the face of Christ in the mural. The emotion and guilt of what he had done flooded him. In one swift movement, he dropped the pack, and knelt before Him. He prayed like he had never prayed before. *I'm sorry, but it was either me or them. I have to get my wife and kids. They are my everything, Lord. Without them, I am nothing. I am so sorry. This is not what I wanted. Please forgive me, oh Lord.* The Lord's Prayer and the Hail Mary poured forth from him, over and over. He prayed. He prayed for his forgiveness and for the safety of his family. He prayed for the souls of the fallen and the rest of humanity. He had never prayed this hard or as much before in his life.

He knelt before the mural of Jesus Christ for some time. Soon, his guilt and remorse abated, as if the clouds parted and the sunlight was allowed to bathe the earth in glory. The weight of his guilt lifted from his heart, *Thank you, Lord,* he thought. He knew that he would carry the consequences of the incident for the rest of his days. He quietly blessed himself with the sign of the cross again and gathered his belongings. With renewed vigor and faith restored he turned eastward and stepped off.

And awaaaay we go. According to my calculations and map, I should be to Janey in about three hours. So, right about noon. Hey Lunch time!

<u>CHAPTER 12</u>

"Any luck?" Jiang-Li shook her head from side to side. They had been wandering the building, testing doors to see which ones were unlocked and which ones weren't. They found that since the power was out, the electric locks basically have the building on lockdown.

"I wonder if there are keys for these doors?" Jiang-Li asked as she slid her fingertips over a keyhole.

"I bet there are and I also bet that Francis has them."

"We should go ask for them, don't you think?"

"No." Janey answered curtly.

"But if he has them, we can open some of these doors and see if anyone else is here."

"No!"

Jiang-Li saw that Janey didn't want to seek out Francis. After what Francis had done to both of them, she thought better of it too. Since the altercation in the market room, they had not seen Francis around. They assumed that he had crawled back to his office and was hiding there. *Good! He can rot in there, for all I care,* Janey thought.

"How many kids do you have?" Jiang-Li asked innocently.

"Two. A boy and a girl." *I thought Jiang-Li knew that!*

"Very nice. I have only one, a boy." *I didn't know that Jiang-Li had a kid.*

"He is grown now, he lives at a college in California. Very far from here." Her voice trailed off, the worry was evident in her tone. Up until now, she hadn't really thought of her own kids. She knew that with all of the time spent in scouts and camping with Jake, her kids would be ok until they got to them. The school they attended had security protocols in place to keep the students safe, at least until Jake and Janey arrived.

"My son, Joey is fourteen and my daughter, Ella, is eleven." *Maybe if I keep talking about my kids it will help keep Jiang-Li's mind off of her own son.*

"Do they do any thing after school?"

"Yes, they do! I already said that Joey is in Boy Scouts, and he is in band. Ella is in Girl Scouts, dance, and gymnastics. She is a busy bee!"

"That is nice. Both in scouts? That sounds like a lot of time driving around."

"Yeah well, Jake is Joey's scout leader and I am Ella's scout leader. So we divide and conquer. Did your son go through scouts?"

"No. He didn't. My husband and I didn't have time to take him. He did play sports in high school, baseball. He was very good at it...."

They continued in silence moving down the corridor checking the doors. They found more doors locked than open and the doors that did open were all useless. A closet with a mop and bucket, or a furnace and boiler room. They even found a private office or two.

"So, Jiang-Li, what does your husband do?" Janey couldn't stand the silence any longer.

"He is an executive for a health care company. He travels very much and he is...." Her voice wavered and Janey could see her lower lip quivering.

"Executive? Wow! Jake is a computer programmer, and he works for a health care company! I wonder if they are the same one."

"Is he a good man?" Jiang-Li stopped and turned to Janey. Their eyes locked and Janey could tell that Jiang-Li was holding a tremendous amount of emotion back. Her deep brown eyes conveyed an unspoken truth. Her husband must have been travelling when the EMP happened. Janey thought of Jake. He wasn't a great man, he was human after all and made mistakes, but he was good to her and the kids. He volunteered at school and with the scouts. He cared for his family to the detriment to his own health sometimes. She smiled.

"Yes. He is a very good man. I don't know what I would do with out him. He is very loving and caring to me and the kids. He would do anything for us. I know that he will make it here." Jiang-Li nodded. She looked at Janey and blurted out.

"I think my husband is dead." The tears flowed freely this time and she stood, unashamed.

"Oh Jiang-Li! You don't know that! He was probably at the airport waiting on his flight-"

"He was in the air over Kansas at that time. He was going to California for work and to visit our son. I couldn't go with him because Francis wouldn't let me take vacation. I should have been with him! I should be dead too!" The strength fled from her legs and she collapsed to the floor.

"Jiang-Li, you don't know that for sure! I bet he is safe-"

" I was tracking his flight with my phone. They have apps for that now! Janey, have you looked at the sky since it happened? Have you? I have and I have not seen a single plane or jet. I haven't even seen the clouds they make! They crashed! I know it!"

Janey was confused. She hadn't been looking at the sky for planes. She had no reason to. *What clouds? Does she mean condensation trails?*

"Jiang-Li, there is no way for you to see every plane or jet or even the condensation trails! We are in a building! You would have to be outside and we haven't gone out there!

"Ok, then let's go see!" She gathered herself up and started back to loading dock area.

"Jiang-Li! Where are you going?"

"To the roof!"

"The roof? How do you know how to get on the roof?" *They were chemists, not facility support staff!* Jiang-Li jogged through the building, Janey had to run to keep up. *I have GOT to start working out!* Unlike Jake, she did not suffer from asthma. Bursting through the last set of doors she collided with Jiang-Li, both were breathy heavily.

"There!" Jiang-Li pointed up at a tall ladder that was mounted on the wall above the catwalk.

"How in the hell are we supposed to get up there? Wait a minute, how do you know all this?"

"I sometimes have lunch with Keith and he took me up there once. It wasn't that great up there, but you can see better."

Keith was facility support staff member that worked in their building. It was a glorified name for maintenance crew. He was responsible for fixing the AC units and clearing out the external vents. He fancied himself a lothario, a player of the game. He had hit on Janey once, telling her that she looked good and asked her if she wanted to have coffee with him. She was flattered but turned him down.

Jiang-Li climbed the metal gratework staircase to the catwalk above. Below them, bathed in shadows, was the stamping area that shared space with the loading dock. Janey followed her up the stairs.

"Well, crap!" The ladder was bolted to the cinder block wall quite securely and was easily reachable from where they stood. The ladder led up fifteen feet to a roof hatch that was closed and latched with a padlock. Jiang-Li smiled and started up the ladder.

"Jiang-Li! Where are going? It's locked, we can't get up there." She didn't respond, and continued climbing. She stopped once she reached the padlock, felt around in her pocket, and produced a single key on a small ring. She went to work on the lock. The lock opened and she pulled it free from the hatch. She left the key in it and let it fall down to the catwalk.

"Look out below!" It narrowly missed Janey. It tumbled through the grating and down into the darkness behind the stamping presses. The small metal mechanism clanged and banged into the darkness.

"Oops! I guess we won't be locking this back up," Jiang-Li looked down at Janey and smiled. It was the first time she had smiled since this had started. Turning her attention back to the hatch, she stepped up and pushed with all her might. The hatch swung up and out, flooding the ladder and catwalk in bright sunlight. The two women were bathed in warm, inviting light. They raised their hands to shield their eyes. The cool fresh air rushed in and overpowered the smell of lubricants and oils. Jiang-Li rushed up and out, with Janey following after.

The roof was covered is small round pieces of stone to help with drainage when it rained. The quietness was terribly unnerving, only broken by the crunching sounds of their footsteps. There were no traffic sounds, the vehicles on the adjacent freeway were not rushing by, no trucks on the main roads, no air conditioner units roaring, nothing!

"It's too quiet. I don't like it." Janey frowned.

"I like it." Jiang-Li turned her face to the sky, absorbing the sunlight like a flower. Janey turned away but also looked to the sky. Both women searched the atmosphere for the tell tale signs of aircraft. Jiang-Li was right, there were no condensation trails from the planes.

"What is that?" Jiang-Li pointed to the south-west. Dark plumes of smoke billowed and climbed high into the air. Something was on fire and there was more than one. They each counted and recounted and then counted again. They couldn't be certain what was burning, but there were twenty-six columns of black smoke. *Car accidents?*

Janey recalled the accident from the day before. She rushed over to the west side of the building that faced MacMillan Highway. The remains of the tractor trailer and car had burned itself out. *That rules out car accidents. What's that smoke coming from then? What is out there?* Janey thought as she made her way back to Jiang-Li.

"Metro Airport." Jiang-Li pointed to the plumes.

Detroit Metro Airport was an international airport with hundreds of planes arriving and departing everyday. It was southwest of them but still close enough that they could see the plumes of smoke.

"It could be car accidents, or buildings on fire." Janey stammered.

"Or planes." Jiang-Li offered quietly.. Janey moved closer to Jiang-Li and put her arm across her shoulders. She looked to the west and thought of Jake and his distance to walk. He had to travel through the cities of Royal Oak, Ferndale, and Farmington. Large urban areas with an equally dense population. Janey looked off to the west where dark clouds were slowing moving towards her. In the distance loud popping noises echoed in on the building wind. *Are those gunshots coming from Royal Oak? Hurry up baby. Be safe, but please hurry.*

<u>CHAPTER 13</u>

The small green street sign up ahead read, Wilcox St. *I've made it quite far and only had the one run in! Lord please don't let me have any more!* Wilcox Street put him less than a mile to his destination and a much needed rest. Jake pressed on, his heart leapt at the thought of finally getting to his wife. A sudden thought shot through his mind, *what if she wasn't there? What if she's walking home?* Excitement, quickly turned to anxiety.

Overhead, the skies in the were full of dark blue and blackish clouds. Mother nature had been insulted by the detonation of a nuclear device and she was building up a come back.

BANG! BANG!

BRRRAAP! BRRRRAP!

The gun shots rang out in rapid succession and Jake could only hope that they were not for him. He ducked behind a work truck for cover. He recalled an old military saying that you never hear the bullet that kills you. *So far, I can still hear them, so I must be alive! Almost there, then on to the kids and then home. HOME!* He sat there a few minutes until the gunshots ceased. He pressed on.

Jake ran through a rough checklist in his head of the meager preparation at home. *Meager! Some might claim them to be, but I know better. I have at least 3 months of food and water. Enough vitamins and first aid supplies to outfit a small pharmacy. Extra dog food for the dogs. The DOGS! I hope they are ok.*

Jake's two beautiful, female Golden Retrievers had been a part of the Hawkins family for many years. Billie was the oldest at fifteen, and had a light golden color to her coat. She had started losing her hearing and sight over the last few months and was affectionately called, The Old Lady. They had gotten her several years after getting married before Joey was born. She was and always would be Jake's favorite.

Samantha, on the other hand, was a six year old dog with dark auburn colored fur. A real beauty but she was quite clingy and loved to go for truck rides with Jake. She never left his side and had intense separation anxiety whenever he left the house.

It had been over twenty-four hours since the pulse and they had been stuck in the house. He was pretty sure that they have knocked over the trash can or nosed into the kitchen pantry looking for food. *They have probably pooped and peed all over the floor too! Poor dogs, I'm coming girls!*

His breathing was becoming heavier and heavier as his pace quickened. A mixture of excitement and anxiety filled him with energy but blinded him to the danger from above.

Suddenly the the sky lit up as if a strobe light was turned on for a few seconds. *Lightning!* He quickly dropped to one knee and started counting.

"One Mississippi, two Mississippi, three Mississippi, four Mississippi…" He counted until the thunder rolled over him.

"…twenty Mississippi." A deep rumble was felt and heard across the silent landscape. He quickly divided by five, and determined that the lightning strike was approximately four miles from his location. *Shit, this storm is going to slow me up. At least I will be in a building when it hits. I hope.*

He started jogging, and really breathing hard now. He internal struggle to grab his inhaler for a puff was overwhelmed by his desire to get to Janey. Just as he neared the four lanes of MacMillan Highway, another flash lit up the sky. Again, he dropped to one knee to count and catch his breath. He leaned heavily on the hiking stick and started counting. *Twenty Mississippi's again. Still four miles away. Good, maybe this storm is moving slow.*

Across the boulevard he saw the sign for her company. The office building sat just beyond it on a small rise. He was here! *Janey!* His heart leapt in his chest at the though of his beloved wife. The ache in his legs and back vanished as he hustled across the street. He wove his way between the destroyed semi and the damaged cars. Reaching the front door, he leaned his hiking stick against the wall and started pounding rhythmically on the glass with his hands and yelling.

"JANEY!! JANEY!! I'M HERE!" He cupped his hands around his face and tried to peer in through the tinted windows. A dark shape darted into one of the offices.

"HEY!! LET ME IN!! HEY! BUDDY! I SAW YOU!
The shape moved again. He continued to shout and pound but still no answer. *Was she even here? Did she stay or did she go?* He remembered that her lab and office was near the rear of the building and she probably was there. He snatched his stick and ran around to the back of the building, huffing and puffing even more now. *I need my inhaler again!* Dark spots began to dance around the corners of his vision as his chest tightened. Fearing that he could black out he forced himself to slow down and control his breathing.

He stopped for a moment under a row of crabapple trees that lined the south side of the building. He dropped the hiking stick, shrugged off his pack and pulled out the inhaler again. Taking two deep breaths of the precious medicine seemed to open the closed airways. The tightness in his chest lessened. *Ahh, relief! Now I can breathe again! If only the pounding in my ears would go away.* He concentrated on slowing his heart rate, and calming his senses now that his breath was under control. *I need to hear more than just the thudding in my ears!* After a few minutes of calming silence and meditation he grabbed his gear and continued on.

Rounding the southeastern corner of the building he could see the rear parking lot. It was scattered with cars but devoid of life. He quickly scanned the rows and saw a familiar maroon vehicle. *Janey's car is still here, so she should still be here, hopefully!* Flash! *One Mississippi, two Mississippi three Mississippi...ten Mississippi.* A nasty crackling sound preceded the rolling thunder. The kind of sound that makes you aware that it was close. So close that the rumble seems to go on forever!

With renewed motivation he ran past the loading dock, to the backdoor of the building and started pounding again and yelling her name. Nothing. *Ok, I guess I have to break my way in.*

Three years ago the building and property owners felt it necessary to add some decorative and aesthetically pleasing features to the otherwise bland industrial property. Features such as apple trees, because of their blossoms, and hydrangia bushes lined the front of the building. Another such addition was a concrete island with a paved sidewalk through the middle, that sat between two of the buildings in the middle of the parking lot. Instead of nice green grass and a picnic table, they chose rocks. A nice sidewalk surrounded by baseball and golfball size rocks. Jake remembered seeing some softball size ones in there while he waited for Janey one day, when they carpooled together. He thought that it was a stupid idea then, but not anymore. He set his pack and stick by the door, and ran for the oasis of rocks.

Flash, flash, flash! No time to count, but he didn't need to, as the thunder came almost instantly. Amidst the rumbling noise, he could have sworn he heard a familiar voice.

"JANEY?" He turned towards the hotel next door, frantically scanning for his beloved wife. He caught a flutter of fabric and flash of yellow from behind one of the few remaining vehicles.

"No!" *I know that yellow, it can't be!*

"Whassup, man?" Yellow Sneakers had found him.

CHAPTER 14

Lightning flashed overhead alerting Janey and Jiang-Li to the approaching storm. Janey looked to the western skies, seeing the dark blue and blackish clouds. She smiled inwardly, thinking of the times that she and her family had called her husband, Jake Gadica. It was combination of his first name and the last name of a famous local weather forecaster, Chuck Gadica. Jake fancied himself an amateur weatherman and she let him.

"We should probably head in," Janey said as she stared at the dark clouds silently moving closer and closer. Thunder rumbled in the distance, followed by another flash of lightning.

"Good idea!" Thunder again rumbled in the distance but it felt much closer. They quickly scampered down the ladder and back into the confines of the oppressive building. Down into the lair of Francis and his lunacy.

"So when did you first come to America, Jiang-Li?" Janey thought that maybe some small talk would help keep their minds off of their husbands.

"About sixteen years ago. My husband, Zhang Wei, is a surgeon and his specialty is in nerves?" Her command of the english language was good, but she still had trouble sometimes.

"He worked at the largest hospital in Beijing but he thought that we could make more money here in the United States. We could have a better life here, than in China."

"So you moved here? What about your son? Did he have a hard time adjusting?" Janey's curiousity was now piqued. They were almost back to the cube farm.

"Yes. We moved all of our belongings from our small house outside of Beijing to here. You would think that being a good doctor would pay good money, but no. It did not. We barely were able to pay for our house and food and clothes for my son. He was excited about the move. He had seen many movies about America and did not have any hard times." She sat down in a chair close to the window while Janey took another one close by. She continued to scan the skies.

"Yeah, but why did you come here?" Francis said, startling them both. They glared at him, narrowing their eyes so tightly that they seemed closed.

"So sixteen years is along time. Did your husband, Zhang, find the success he was hoping for?" Janey turned back to Jiang-Li.

"Yes, but not at first…"

"Well of course not, at first!" Francis interjected.

"Ignore him, Jiang-Li. Please, go on." She glared at him, with daggers and hate in her eyes.

"He did not, but we had just come here, and we did not have much money. He worked as an intern, just as in China after medical school, and after a few years he had been promoted to his former position. Six more years and he was in charge of his department! Money was important in China, we saved and saved when we lived there. But here we soon had more than we could spend! You see, we had to save all the money to buy just food and clothes, but here! My goodness, the food was cheaper and there was so much of it! We have a really nice house now and we don't worry about food anymore!" She smiled at Janey.

"What about your son? Was he able to fit in at school? I hope he didn't have any trouble with the other kids," she probed gently.

"I bet he had a hell of a hard time! Probably couldn't speak any English, only Chinese! Probably got picked on a lot!" Francis relished in the thought of her son getting bullied.

"FRANCIS, SO HELP ME GOD IF YOU DON'T SHUT THE HELL UP, I WILL BEAT YOUR ASS AGAIN!" The sudden outburst shocked both him and Jiang-Li. He sneered at them as he shrank back into the shadows again.

"Sorry about that Jiang-Li. He can be such an asshole!"

"Thank you, Janey." She smiled meekly.

"How did your son handle the transition?"

"Very well in fact. Remember I said he watched a lot of American movies? Well he learned a good deal of english from them and when we came here, he made many friends." The two women continued to talk about their kids and their accomplishments. Both proud of the people their children were becoming.

The storm had crept closer and closer. The lightning flashed brighter and more frequently. The thunder had drowned their voices out and conversation waned. They both stared out the windows at the oncoming storm.

"I hope my dog is ok, he doesn't like storms," Jiang-Li said. *DOGS!*

"Oh shit! I hope my dogs are ok too! I hadn't even thought of them till now!" Images of light and dark fur, flashing tongues and wagging tails dashed through her mind.

"You have dogs too?" Jiang-Li asked.

"Yes, two girls. We call them our fur-babies. Billie and Samantha. Samantha is our youngest baby at six years old and she has the most beautiful dark caramel fur and it's so soft!! Billie is our oldest baby. We actually got her before we had my son! She is fifteen years old now." Her heart suddenly was very heavy for the old girl, this whole situation could be too much for her. *Oh God, I hope they are ok!*

"What kind of dog do you have," Janey asked.

"Oh, Shatzi? He is a Pomeranian, with soft light brown fur. He is a little tense sometimes and storms make him scared. He will go under my bed to hide from the thunder." Her eyes began to tear up as she thought of her beloved pet.

"I have two cats. Total assholes. Usually crap in my shoes if I don't feed them on time." They both slowly turned toward Francis, their eyes narrowed with disdain. He could feel their hate and anger like a thousand little bees stinging him at once. He scratched his arms absentmindedly.

"Whatever, I'm gonna check out the front of the building, if you even care." He turned away from the women, and skulked off.

Why don't they like me? I try to fit in with them and they just get mad at me? Francis's thoughts were filled with self angst and despair. *They used to like me, I remember the Christmas parties and lunch times when we all used to laugh and pal around. What happened?* Before he realized it he was standing at the door to the lobby. Two sets of heavy tinted glass doors separated him from the outside. The interior of the foyer was very dark, and he could barely see the world beyond. The dark clouds had almost completely blotted out the sunlight. Another peal of thunder shook the walls, but this time it didn't stop. THUDTHUDTHUD, THUD, THUD, THUD, THUDTHUDTHUD! *That's not thunder, it's rhythmic! SOS?* The pounding repeated again, same as before. Squinting his eyes, he stepped closer to the door and grasped the bar. He gently pushed it down and prepared to step forward. He stopped when he saw a tall, male form loaded with a backpack illuminated by an intense lightning flash.

"JANEY!? JANEY! ARE YOU IN THERE!" The voice startled Francis out of his revere. *JAKE! He's here! Oh shit, he made it!* He released his grip on the bar and stepped back. Jake pressed his face up to the glass, trying to see in. *I don't think he can see me.*

"Hey Buddy! I see you! Let me in!" Jake had seen Francis but he didn't recognize him. Seeking cover, he stepped back and dove into small office.

After a few minutes the pounding and yelling had stopped. Carefully, Francis peeked out and saw that Jake had disappeared. *Oh shit, oh shit, oh shit! What if he did see me? What if he tells Janey that I didn't let him in!* His anxiety skyrocketed at the thought. *I have to find them!*

119

He rushed back to where his two subordinates were when he left them, but they were gone.

"SHIT!" *They must have heard that asshat pounding on the windows! THE BACK DOOR!* He ran back to the rear entrance, hoping to be the first to let Jake in, and be the hero.

He was too late.

================== * ==================

THUDTHUDTHUD, THUD, THUD, THUD, THUDTHUDTHUD.

"Hey, do you here something?" Jiang-Li cocked her head to one side, listening intently. The thumping continued. *SOS!*

"JAKE!! He's here!" Janey jumped up and took off for the rear door.

"What?! He is? How do you know?" Jiang-Li was straining to keep up.

"It's an SOS, a message to me!" They reached the door and before she could open it, Jiang-Li cut her off.

"NO! It might be a trick!" Janey tried to push past her friend. But Jiang-Li held her back.

"Let's just peek outside and see if we can see if he is here." She pointed at the small security window. Janey nodded and stepped up to the small window that looked out on the lot. She had to stand on her tiptoes to get a good look. She immediately spotted her own car and standing next to it was her husband!

"JAKE!! He's here!" She pushed the door wide open and screamed!

"JAKE! I'M HERE!" He didn't hear her. The storm was upon them and the thunder had drowned her out. He hadn't even turned to look at her. *Why is he looking at the hotel? He's talking to someone, who?* A big, white panel van blocked her view of the other person. But she could clearly see Jake pull a handgun out of his waist band from the small of his back and then duck down behind her car. *What the hell is going on! Where did he get that gun?*

KABLAM!

"JAKE!!" She screamed out again and this time he saw her. He turned to her and yelled back.

"JANEY! GET BACK INSIDE! TAKE COVER!" He shucked off the backpack and fell to all fours. He crawled around the front of the car.

KABLAM! KABLAM!

"NO!! she screamed.

CHAPTER 15

Mother-Pusbucket! I knew I should have taken that asshole out when I had the chance. The event that had occurred will take him long time to recover from. The coming times were going to be different. No more jails, no more courts, no more trial by due process, no more guilty until proven innocent. It will only be the law of nature. Kill or be killed.

No, now I have some scumbag trying to kill me! Jake had ducked down behind his wife's car, hoping that it was thick enough to shield him. His wife was so close now, he could almost feel her presence. He checked the handgun, fully loaded, clicked off the safety and peeked over the hood.

KABLAM!

The round ricocheted off the hood, causing paint to fly and his ears to start ringing. He ducked back down again. *SHIT!*

"JAKE!" Janey yelled again. He glanced back to the building and saw her being restrained by an asian woman and a man standing motionless behind them.

KABLAM! KABLAM! Cement and paint exploded from the wall next to the doorway.

"JANEY! GET BACK! GET INSIDE AND STAY THERE!" he yelled and waved them back as they fell back into the vestibule. The door automatically closed behind them. He hoped that the door was thick enough to shield them from any harm.

"THAT YOUR BITCH? I'MA TREAT HER REAL GOOD, YA KNOW?" Sneakers was taunting Jake, trying to get a rise out of him and maybe make a fatal mistake. *Fat chance, asshole.* Jake raised his head to look through the passenger side window, he still hadn't seen where the punk was shooting from. KABLAM!

The window shattered into thousands of tiny pieces and rained down onto him.

"C'MON YOU HONKEY MUTHAFUCKA! STICK YO SHINY WHITE HEAD UP! I'M FITTIN TO BUST IT WIDE OPEN!"

"Jesus, won't this guy shut up!" Jake said under his breath. *How many shots was that? I think he might be low and ready to reload, ok, this is gonna be stupid and reckless, but here goes.* One more time Jake raised his head up to peer through the now shattered window. KABLAM! KABLAM! KABLAM! Click!

"SHIT!" The punk lowered the gun and started frantically trying to eject the magazine.

"YOU SHOULDA KILLED ME WHEN YOU HAD THE CHANCE! YOU KILLED MY BRUTHAS BUT YOU DIDN'T DO ME! YOU SHOULDN'T A DONE THAT! THAT WAS YOUR MISTAKE, ASSHOLE!" He screamed as he jammed the fresh magazine home.

"NOW I'M GETTING EVEN!" He stepped out from the cover of the van, and started walking towards the little red Escape that had shielded his prey.

"Where you hidin at? Did I get you?" He cautiously advanced. Jake was frantically trying to think of something to do or say to make this guy back off but he had nothing. A scene from a movie flashed in his mind. *I hope this works,* he thought as laid flat on the ground and sighted the bright yellow sneakers advancing on the car. He squeezed the trigger once and then twice, sending two tiny pieces of metal at his targets: shinbones! They tore through the jeans, skin and bone in the time it took for Jake to blink.

"AAAHHHAH!!" The punk dropped to the ground and instinctively grabbed for his wounds. The gun fell from his hands and skittered several feet away. Jake leapt to his feet, scooped up the gun and stood over his assailant.

"You should have left me alone. I didn't want to do this. I just want to get home to my kids. I hoped you had changed your mind."

"FUCK YOU, I HOPE YOU FUCKING ROT IN HELL!" He held his legs tightly as blood seeped between his fingers.

"I'm sorry, but you brought this on yourself. May God forgive me and may he forgive you as well." He raised the punks' gun and squeezed the trigger once more. KABLAM!

The last thing that went through the thugs mind was another tiny piece of metal, changing it permanently.

CHAPTER 16

Together at Last

The sight of her husband being attacked and shot at, came as a terrible shock to Janey. She wanted to run out there and help him. She knew next to nothing about guns, but in the face of absolute violence and death, she was willing to learn. She had handled a 22. rifle and even fired a .410ga shotgun, but never a handgun. Still, she was fighting to get out and help. Thankfully her co-worker had a cooler head. Jiang-Li wrestled her back into the building and secured the door.

"You can't go out there! You could be killed!" Jiang-Li begged.

"I don't care! That's my husband and I have to help him!" She tried to push past Jiang-Li, but this time Francis was there.

"Jiang-Li, maybe we should let her go. She might be able to help him." His eyes were glassed over and he didn't sound right to her. Even Janey took notice.

KABLAM! KABLAM! KABLAM!

"Come, this way, we can see what is going on from the labs!" Jiang-Li gently pulled on Janey's arm, guiding her away from the door and Francis. They ran to the north end of the building, past the metal working lab, which had no windows except the skylight. They made it the offices just in time to see a young black man with bright yellow sneakers, walking slowly towards Janey's car. The same car that Jake's was crouched behind. She still couldn't see him, but she did notice the windows had been shot through. That made her sad, *aw man, that was a new car! OH JAKE! Where are you?*

BANG! BANG! More shots rang out, but it wasn't from the young black man, he had fallen to the ground and was clutching his lower legs. His jeans were now turning a bright red color under his fingers. He was screaming at Jake and flailing about. A figure quickly rose from behind the maroon vehicle and dashed towards the fallen shooter, but did not provide aid. He crouched down and picked up another gun.

"JAKE!" He's safe! Oh thank God!" She hugged Jiang-Li. They watched as the two warriors spoke to each other. Janey was feeling elated that her husband was safe. He had come for her, and he had protected her. He was a shining beacon of hope for her and the kids.

KABLAM! She looked up and saw him lowering the gun, and the shooter no longer moving. Then he made the sign of the cross and crouched down over the now still body. *Did he just kill that guy? Oh. My. GOD! What did he just do? I didn't think he was capable of taking a human life! But if Jake didn't do that then he would have been killed and maybe worse for me!* Janey was both shocked and relieved. She smiled at Jiang-Li as she ran to the back door and flung it wide open.

"JAKE!" He turned to the sound of her voice and smiled, his eyes blurred with tears as he ran to her.

"JANEY!" Finally together, they embraced tightly and warmly. They pulled back slightly and kissed each other tenderly. Jiang-Li and Francis stood in the vestibule, in shock from the violence they had just witnessed. He came to his senses as Jake and Janey started towards them. He slunk back into the shadows of the dock and disappeared.

Janey and Jake hurried back to the entranceway, holding each other's hands, never letting go.

"Are you okay?" They both asked at the same time. He chuckled and gestured to her.

"You go first," he said.

"Yeah, I think so."

"Did you get the bag from the car?" he queried.

"Yes, I did. Yesterday, thank you." She answered sheepishly.

"Ok, now, are you alright? What just happened? Who was that guy? What did he want?" She peppered him with questions, and he swallowed hard, readying for the answers. He opened his mouth to speak but any answer he might have had was quickly washed away by the roaring sound of the wind as it picked up speed. The storm was here.

"Let's get inside and I'll tell you all about it!" They hurried inside, pausing only once to grab his pack and stick. Once inside the safety of the building, he realized that his hands were shaking again. Thinking quickly, he shoved them into his pockets. *I hope nobody saw that!*

They hurried to the conference room as it was on the west side of the office building and gave them a good view of the storm as it railed about outside. Jake leaned his hiking stick against the door jam, and set his pack on a chair. He looked up once at Janey.

"Honey, where is your stuff, we have to go. NOW!" He was rifling through his pack.

"Is there anyone else here besides you and Jiang-Li?"

"Yeah, why?" her brows furrowed in confusion.

"Well, I was at the front entrance banging on the doors and windows."

"We heard you." They smiled as they remembered the joy they felt at his arrival.

"Yeah, well, someone was there, I couldn't make out who, just a male figure."

"Maybe it was Francis," she said.

"Francis?" he asked. He stopped his rifling and looked out the door way. His face twisted in anger.

"Yep." All of the anger and rage that had built up over the years of torment he had put his beloved wife through came bubbling to the surface. His balled fists trembled. Janey wrapped her arms around his waist and leaned her head against his chest. His heart thumped wildly, but started to slow. He looked down at her and tried to smile, but she only saw anger and sadness. He pulled back from her and continued going through his pack.

"Francis," he scowled and growled through gritted teeth. He looked back to Janey.

"Get your stuff, please. Jiang-Li go with her."

"You still didn't answer my questions! Are you okay? What just happened? Who was that guy? What did he want?" He closed his eyes, took in a deep breath, and let it out slowly.

"Ok, one question at a time. Take me to where your gear is and let me sit down for a minute. I'll answer you while you pack up."

"Well, hello there!" A male voice from the shadows caused all of them to jump. Francis stepped into the faint light, revealing himself. He held his hands out palms showing almost as if to say that he was not a threat. He quickly noticed that Jake was scowling at him. Francis extended his hand for Jake to shake as a gentlemanly greeting. Jake looked down at it, then slowly looked back up at Francis. He did not shake it. Francis coughed and awkwardly lowered his hand.

"Thank you, for coming for us! We were just getting ready to leave, then this storm came upon us." Francis stammered. Jake stood before him and glared. He took in another deep breath and spoke softly.

"I only came for Janey, you can go spit for all I care." Janey took Jake by the hand and guided him deeper into the building. He pointed to her now abandoned office, and she told him that they only have a couple of flashlights and candles left. She reminded him that there were no windows in her office space. Jake saw that Francis followed along like a lost puppy trailing behind the pack. But this puppy was capable of nipping and causing pain.

"Hey, we need your help. Some of us want to get home too! " Francis called out to the group. Jake stopped and turned on him, his face contorted up in anger.

"Really, Francis? Really? You're a grown man, right? You don't know the way home? Does your mom drop you off and pick you up everyday? If you do know the way home, what is stopping you from going right now? Could it be that you're a coward? Hm?" Jake asked him rhetorically.

"Well, I think..."

"I don't give a flying fuck what you think! You are a waste of space! A dickless, spineless, worthless, piece of human scum that isn't worth my time! GET LOST!" Francis slowly backed away from Jake, his eyes as wide as saucers.

"Yeah, that's right, slink back to the hole that you came out of! Don't push me Francis, I assume you saw me kill a man just a few minutes ago. I would not push the man that did that! He might not have any qualms about killing again!"

Francis now shocked and defeated, turned and left. Jiang-Li and Janey stood behind Jake, supporting their new hero. After the outburst, Jake turned back to the women and smiled.

"What happened to his nose?" He asked Janey. She quickly brought him up to speed on what happened with them. He smiled broadly and swept her into a tight hug, *that's my girl!*

"I'm sorry, you are Jiang-Li, right?" He asked. She smiled and nodded.

"Yes, I am Jiang-Li Chen. I work with your wife, and she has been helping me. Thank you , Jake," she said as she shook his hand.

"You are most welcome, Mrs. Chen..."

"Jiang-Li, please, " she interjected.

"Jiang-Li, will you excuse us for second, I'd like to talk to my wife privately. But don't wander too far!" She nodded her understanding and moved out of earshot. Satisfied that they were relatively alone, he turned back to Janey and he asked what the story was with Jiang-Li. Janey explained that Jiang-Li's husband was on a business trip and his flight may have gone down somewhere in Kansas. Her son was a college student and lived out of state.

"She doesn't have anyone local to help her. I was thinking she could come with us."

"Does she live on the east side of town, like, on the way home?"

"No, she lives in Ann Arbor." He rubbed the bridge of his nose in frustration.

"Ok, honey you know that I have been preparing for most, if not all eventualities and we are not prepared to have another mouth to feed when we get home! That is IF we make it home! Hell, we won't have enough to just get home with her." Janey gave him that look, sort of a pleading, puppy dog look, but it also conveyed that she meant business.

"Fine, but I don't think this is a good idea. What does Jiang-Li think? Have you talked to her about this?"

"Not yet, but I think she wants to leave here and stay with someone familiar."

"I would love to come along! Mr. Jake, I promise I will do what ever you ask and I won't eat much. I promise that I will not be a burdon to you or Janey." She had been eavesdropping the whole time. He looked back and forth at each of them. Their pleading eyes melted his cold heart.

"OK, but we need to go soon! Janey, get your pack and Jiang-Li get your personal stuff. If you have more comfortable shoes to change into, I would do so." They broke up and gathered their belongings, while Jake checked and rechecked his gear. He calculated that with Jiang-Li coming home they would have less than three months of food and water amongst all of them. He would have to come up with some ways to replenish their stores quicker than he had hoped. He stood up and stretched his spine and spied a water fountain across the office space. He grabbed his empty bottles and decided to test his luck. He said a silent prayer and gave the handle a twist. Success! There was still enough pressure in the lines to fill his bottles, and his camelpack bladder. Just enough.

"All, set!" Janey called out.

"Great, we need to get moving!" Shouldering their packs, they made it to the door, when Mother Nature decided to play her trump card. The clouds that had been carrying the rain, finally opened up, spilling their contents over the city. The deluge could only have been equal to the rains that Noah and his ark dealt with. *Great, just freakin' great,* he thought.

CHAPTER 17

The weather, up to the last few hours, had been cooperating nicely, but not anymore. The storm had struck with tremendous force. The rain came down so hard and fast that the drains in the parking lot were erupting like geysers from the amount of air trying to escape the sewer depths.

Thankfully the storm didn't last long. Soon the thunder and lightning had started to abate and the rain had diminished into a drizzle. The clouds had begun to thin, allowing the sunlight to break through. It cast a bit of light into the darkened office complex. Jake had the women bring their gear to an open cube next to the windows for better viewing.

Janey had also brought the backpack that Jake had packed for her. Each women set their purse on the table alone with their laptops and accessories. He opened each bag and slid the laptops out.

"Well, you won't be needing these anymore," he said as he tossed them over the wall of the cube. The women were both shocked and elated. The once expensive devices crashed against the desks on the other side of the wall and then fell to the floor, screens cracked and keys went flying. The devices that Francis had figuratively shackled to them since day one, were no more. He smiled and winked at them playfully.

"I've always wanted to do that!" The power cords and accessories soon met the same fate.

He continued going through their belongings, carefully asking permission before he opened their purses. Satisifed that he had weeded out the useless items and junk, he gave them each a handwritten list of items to search for. Water, food stuffs, personal hygiene products and batteries were at the top of each list.

Francis had crept back into the area. Keeping his head down and moving slowly, he was trying to get close enough to hear what their plans were. He settled into a cube not far away, but close enough to hear them. He sat down and relaxed for a moment, just as the computers came flying over the wall. He lunged toward them but was in no position to catch them. He watched helplessly as the expensive company property crashed to the floor and splinter into pieces. *No, no, no, no, no! I am going to be in so much trouble! I am in charge of the equipment for my department and upper management will have my head for this, this, this wanton destruction by a non-employee! He doesn't even work here! He is trespassing!*

"Ok, I want to be out of here as soon as the rain lets up. If you have a coat or jacket, get it now because it's looking better out there." Jake had unfurled a map that he pulled from his pack and was staring at it intently.

After a few minutes of sitting in silence, Francis slunk back to his own office to make his own preparations to leave. *If they won't take me with them, then I might just have to follow along. But at a safe distance.* He was so deep in thought that he didn't notice the small trashcan jutting out into the aisle between cubes. His foot connected with it and sent it spinning down the aisle. *CLANG!* The sound of the can crashing in the twilight of the office was like a herd of cattle stampeding in a cave. He dropped to the ground and scampered after it, hoping that they didn't hear it. *Who could have been so stupid to leave their trashcan in the walkway! I'm gonna find out whose cube that is and they are going to have to answer for their clumsiness and stupidity and lackadaisical attitudes. This will definitely be going in my report about this whole cockamamie thing!*

Francis was so upset about the placement of the can, and what he was going to do to the employee, that he didn't hear Jake approaching from behind. He grabbed Francis by the shirt and pushed him hard into the wall. Jake advanced slowly, fists clenched.

"What are doing, Francis?" Jake demanded, his eyes flashed with anger.

"Nothing. Leave me alone." His eyes wide with fear, darted back and forth, searching for an exit.

"Nothing my ass! You have done nothing but harass and demean my wife since the day you took over as her boss! You mistreat her, and everyone in your department! You know what, I'm done with you and more importantly, SHE is done with you" he pointed to Janey.

"You won't last ten minutes out in the world now because you are weak and a coward. You only know how to boss people around to make you look good to your own bosses, well, where are they now? Surely they're coming for you, right? No. They're not. No one is and no one will."

"They may not be coming for me, but I will make sure that this building and all inside it are safe and secure. I will be rewarded for my service and you will be going to jail for destruction of property!" Francis spat back.

"Who gives a flying fuck about this building! You know what? I am done wasting time on you. You are just a waste of space, a drain on humanity. Goodbye and fuck off!" Jake turned to leave.

Francis had had enough of the physical and verbal abuse. Roaring like a caged animal he launched himself at Jake's legs. The move caught Jake off guard and they tumbled to the ground, in a tangle of arms and legs. He quickly tried to gain the upper hand over his opponent. He flipped Jake over and climbed on top, smacking Jake's head and face ineffectually. The blows glanced off the top of Jake's head with almost no force and no damage.

He reached down to the gun tucked in Jake's waistband and they grappled more furiously for the treasured item. Whoever had that gun had control, and Francis wanted control. He wanted it so badly he could taste it.

The gun came loose, and Francis gripped it tightly, but incorrectly. He wasn't about to let it go, but his strength was waning. They fought harder, but Jake was stronger than he was. Jake twisted his wrist, freeing the gun. It fell to the floor and bounced into the dark cubes. He punched Francis in the face, smashing his already broken nose, blinding him with pain. Enraged, he redoubled his efforts, punching and scratching. Jake was quicker, he jabbed and poked Francis in the eyes. He screamed out in pain as Jake rolled him off and regained his footing. Realizing that he was losing the fight, he screamed and lunged again, but this time Jake saw it coming. He boxed Francis's' ears, once, twice, three times. Francis screamed with each blow, this time in pain and defeat. He fell to the floor, holding the sides of this head, crying in shame.

Jake picked up the gun from where it had to come to rest and leveled it at Francis.

"JAKE! STOP!" Jiang-Li had heard the commotion and had come running. Janey had witnessed the encounter with fear and awe. Without taking his eyes off of Francis, Jake said calmly.

"We are leaving. You are NOT to follow. If I see you again, you will be put down like the mangy dog you are. Do you understand me?"

Francis glared back at him, blood poured from his nose again.

"I said, do you understand me?" Again, the glare was all Jake received.

"Fine, have it your way." He pulled the slide back on the handgun and chambered a round, switched the safety off and levelled the gun at Francis again.

"Yes, I understand," he growled. Without lowering the weapon, Jake instructed the women to get their gear and his, then meet him outside the front entrance. They turned and left, *probably talking about me,* Francis thought. The two men glared back at each other, neither one happy about the situation.

"If my wife hadn't stopped me, I want you to know, I would have done it," Jake said as he lowered the gun. Making it safe, he turned and left Francis to lick his wounds. Francis sat on the floor, defeated. He watched them go, fading into the darkness of the cubes.

"You will see me again. I guarantee it, and next time it will be YOU who will be the dogs!" he spat at them.

=================== * ===================

"What about Francis?" Jiang-Li asked him as they were leaving. Jake looked to Janey and without a word between them being said, they agreed.

"Fuck him." With that, they left her company and Francis behind. Forever.

CHAPTER 18

The lightning and thunder had moved eastward and was fading fast. The rain had washed the world into a new day and a new time. The drains had started to catch up to the standing water in the gutters and low areas. The standing pools of water had begun to diminish.

The smell of a good rain always seemed to have a calming effect on Jake. The trio stood outside the front entrance of the building. He closed his eyes and took several deep breaths through his nose while the women slung their backpacks and gear. Jiang-Li had found someone's gym bag in her search for items on her list. It had been emptied and inspected. It stunk a little bit, but it was far better and bigger than her laptop bag or purse.

"Ready?" Janey asked him as she adjusted the straps on her pack. He looked at her and smiled, then to Jiang-Li.

"Yes."

"How far is it to get home?"

"About twenty miles to your mom's house."

"Shouldn't we go home first? The kids might be there."

"I'm hoping that there was some lead time before this all started. I didn't get any calls from the school, did you?"

"No, I don't think so. You know I don't get service in the lab and since I can't check it now…"

"I hope that the school got ahold of your mom and she was able to get them to her house. If not, at least we can check on her, since her house is on the way home." Janey's mother was the first emergency contact listed in case of emergency. *He had thought this whole thing through. Even though we are so far from home, and without the kids, he is thinking of my mom too! I couldn't love him more than I do right now*, she thought.

"Let's get going!" She said as she started towards MacMillan Highway. He didn't follow her. Jiang-Li looked from Jake to Janey, not knowing which way to go. Janey realized that he wasn't following her. She stopped and turned back to him.

"What?" He smiled and jerked his thumb over his shoulder.

"I'm going this way, over the freeway." He pointed towards the highway.

"What? We can't cross the interstate!"

"Why not? It's not like we will be hit by a car! There are no cars or trucks moving." He went her, took a breath and rested his hands on her shoulders.

"Honey, listen to me, the roads and paths that we will be taking will be across parking lots, through yards and fields. There should be no one to stop us, and we need to avoid the more heavily populated areas. My maps have us crossing here and skirting the mall. Once we are northeast of here we will be walking on sidewalks and cutting through some subdivisions. Ultimately we will be stopping at a small park to sleep in."

"Why do we have to avoid the mall? Who are we trying to avoid?"

"Looters. Thugs. Hoodlums. Bad guys. Think back to all that footage we saw of the last hurricane that blew through. Remember all of the looting and rioting that went on during power outages in the south? It's gonna happen here too." The encounter in the rear parking lot of her building flashed in her mind.

"Bad guys, yeah, right. Ok, I'll follow you."

"How will we know what the bad guys look like?" Jiang-Li asked, joining the conversation.

"When you see them, you'll know," he answered. She nodded and together they stepped out into the new world.

As they crossed the interstate, Janey remarked that it was too eerie. There were hundreds of vehicles, some with people still milling about, thinking that they will start working again magically or protecting what they considered valuable property. Other vehicles had clearly been abandoned, their doors and trunk lids hung open. None of the people called out to them or even really noticed them. Jake thanked the Lord for small miracles.

They continued moving eastward across parking lots and behind department stores. Their journey together had an uneventful start and Jake was grateful, but it was not to last. BRRRAAAP! BANG! BANG! BRRRAAP!

"Shit! Get down!" he ordered.

"Is that the bad guys?" Jiang-Li asked fearfully.

"Yes, I think so. It's coming from the mall. Only two miles in and now this."

The looters were in high gear, taking anything that looked valuable and wasn't bolted down. Jake had hoped to avoid this, but they need to step up their pace. They crouched behind cars, trucks, and used buildings for cover, hoping to avoid being spotted. Jake told them to get behind him and go where he goes.

Across the four lane highway and vast parking lot sat a popular department store and an electronics store, both of which had a large group of people gathered in front. The voices were just a cacophony of sound, no one voice was louder than the others. Janey thought they sounded angry. The only discernable sound was of breaking glass. *Even though there is no power some people want their a big screen TV or laptop. Great.* Jake turned to them.

"Ok, we will continue on. Walk normal, do not run! It will only draw attention to us, and no matter what, do NOT make eye contact with anyone. These folks are not prepared and may try to take what we have. I can't possibly take on that many people. We need to get away from this area as soon as we can." They nodded their agreement to follow him. Jiang-Li was visibly upset, but was holding it together, for now.

CHAPTER 19

The almost abandoned building held only silence for the lone occupant. The inky blackness of the shadows was growing in the small cubicles and offices. Another kind of darkness was also growing in the man's heart and mind. He had watched the trio of survivors leave through the front entrance and then tracked their movements from   inside. The tinted windows gave him cover and a sense of security. He watched them as they circled back behind the building and out of sight. He made his way back to his office and sat down in the darkness. He sat alone for what seemed like hours but was only minutes.

"You are better than them, Francis." A hushed voice whispered. Francis whipped his head around, looking for the source.

"Who said that? Who's here?" He commanded. His heart pounded in his chest.

"You are not a coward, or a weakling." The voice continued.

"Where are you? I demand to know who is speaking!" His voice cracked in terror.

"You know who it is. Get up now and get going!"
He fell back into his chair, his eyes wide open. His heart slowed and a glassy look came over him.

"Yes, I think I know." He answered robotically.

"They are getting away!" The internal voice encouraged him further.

"They left you here to rot. They disobeyed you. They threatened you. HE destroyed company property!" It hissed in his ear. It continued to fuel his anger and hatred of the deserters and that interloper, Jake.

"Good, good! Now get your stuff. Just the essentials now." The disembodied voice pushed him along further.

"Ok." He said aloud. His voice was flat and emotionless.

Francis gathered his own belongings; his laptop and bag, a few folders of important documents and his metal water bottle with the company logo emblazoned on the side.

"Hurry up, they are getting away! We need to punish them!" Francis hurried through the office building pausing only to lock the doors behind him. He wanted to make sure that when the power came back he might be rewarded for his deeds. The rear entrance few open and Francis emerged into the gloomy daylight.

He ran through the parking lot and along the side of the rear buildings that lined the interstate. His tan overcoat, now stained with dots of moisture, flapped in the breeze.

"Where are they going? There is no way out back there?" he wondered aloud. He skidded to a halt at the edge of the building, his loafers provided little grip on the mud and dirt. He dropped to the ground and hoped that they hadn't seen him. He watched quietly as the group reached the fencing between the parking lot and the interstate. Their leader, bent down and lifted the fence up while the women crawled under. He watched them cautiously jump over the puddles of standing water and climb the embankment to the highway. The dogs were getting away, and the fear of losing them washed over him! He watched his enemies as they walked across the interstate to freedom. He grabbed his bag, and stood up, not bothering to wipe the mud and dirt himself off.

He stepped out of from behind the building and stepped into the wet grass. A feeling of satisfaction that he would be rewarded for his actions washed over him.

"Did you leave the note?" The hushed voice asked. A sudden jolt of anxiety shot through him. He thought back to his movements inside and remembered that he had left a note for his boss, just in case the world righted itself, just like he knew it would.

"Yes, I left it."

"Good job, Francis. You are an excellent employee"

"Thank you."

He ran for the spot in the fence where he watched the group climb under and through. He lifted the fence, kicked his bag through, and followed after. He emerged onto the interstate and gasped at the site.

"They are getting away, Francis. They musn't get away! They need to be punished for destroying the property!"

"Where did they go?" He said to no one in particular. His dark hair, once coifed and styled perfectly now hung in wet tangles on his head. Pieces of tree and bush were stuck in the dripping mess.

"Hey man, are you looking for your friends?" A tall middle-aged man, still dressed for his white collar job stepped out from behind a luxury sedan.

"He knows where they went, say something."

"Yeah, did you see which way they went?" He answered the stranger.

"Who?"

"THEM! THEM! A MAN AND TWO WOMEN! WHERE DID THEY GO?" His voice exploded from him, startling the Samaritan. The man nodded his understanding and pointed east across the interstate and towards the mall. He retreated to the safety of his sedan.

BRRRAAAP! BANG! BANG! BRRRAAP! The gunshots rang out from the direction the man was directing him to go.

"They were going towards the mall, I think. But, I'd steer clear if I was you." He jumped into the open car and slammed the door.

"Thank him." The voice directed once again.

"Thanks!" The man in the car watched Francis walk briskly away, thankful for the safety of the vehicle.

Francis' eyes darted back and forth, scanning the area for the trio. He spied several groups scattered about, but they weren't wearing packs or they were the wrong combination of men and women. Soon he saw three familiar people, with gear.

"IT'S THEM!" The voice was louder now. He had caught up to the pack of dogs.

He followed a short distance behind them, stopping everytime they stopped, moving when they moved. He saw them turn left and walk nonchalantly down the middle of the street, weaving between the vehicles. He glanced at the street sign, John R. Road.

He blinked a few times to make sure that he wasn't seeing things. They were walking up the center of John R. Road! *A five lane highway, full of cars and trucks, and they were walking along like they owned the road! The audacity!* He thought.

He was so full of malice and hate that he almost didn't see the young hoodlum come out of the entrance to the store he was hiding next to. The young man stepped out of the entrance and leveled a small handgun at Francis. Francis glared at him with a level of crazy that this young man had never seen before. His eyes were glassy and far away. The young man's eyes darted back and forth, trying to see if this guy had any friends or back around.

"Ok." Francis said aloud to himself and nodded.

"What? I didn't say thing man!" Before the hoodlum could say any more Francis lunged for the weapon. They struggled for a few seconds, but Francis emerged victorious. It was the second time that he had to struggle for a weapon that day and he wasn't about to lose. Again.

The young man took off running. No more words were spoken, no shots fired. But now Francis had a gun. *See*, he thought, *that is how it is done. Law and Order, Right and Wrong. These are the ways of the world, my world.* He would make them see the ways of his world. He watched the dirty, rotten, "pack of dogs" continue north down the road.

CHAPTER 20

The further north they went, the easier it became to travel unnoticed. The shopping centers were full of people, looting and pillaging, but if they avoided them, they would be okay. The streets had dried and the skies were clear once again. The grass was still wet, and appeared to be coated in dew, but that would soon be dried.

The women spied a jogging and hiking store and asked if they should also try to get some better belongings. Before Jake could answer, the sound of gunshots and screaming answered for him. They continued north, crossing Big Beaver Road. and into high dollar country. The houses had now become mansions and they started to get bigger and bigger. Gated communities greeted them along the way. They continued on, ignoring the dwellings of the people who were more interested in monetary wealth instead of spiritual or intellectual wealth.

"Could we stop for a break soon?" Janey asked, her face was flushed and sweat dripped down her nose. Jake pulled a handkerchief from his back pocket and gently blotted her face and brow. He planted a quick kiss on her nose and smiled.

"Yes, please, my feet are too sore." Jiang-Li grimaced. Jake paused, looked at them both and nodded. *It will give me a chance to check the map,* he thought.

"There is a park up ahead called Raintree Park and we can take an extended break when we arrive. It's about a half hour more to get there, but we can rest for five minutes here. Only five minutes!" He insisted and they agreed. He handed his hiking stick to Jiang-Li to use as support and to take her mind off of her aching feet.

"There it is, Raintree Park!" Jiang-Li exclaimed, pointing out a green and brown sign. Jake glanced at his watch, thirty minutes. *Damn, I'm good,* he thought. It was a small city park, with a baseball diamond, and a couple of port-a-potties. Short maple trees lined the municipal meadow.

Outside the park they stopped. Jake looked it over, scanning for any occupants, good or bad. He pointed to a large grouping of trees and told them to head for it.

"Walk fast, but don't run, we don't want any unwanted attention." He said softly. He was acutely aware that with no road noise to drown them out, their voices carried. They nodded and headed off toward the stand of poplars and pines. The two women moved calmly and quickly, covering the distance in no time. Janey turned back to Jake and gave him a thumbs up sign. Satisfied that they made it safely to cover, he turned his attention back to the roadway. He wanted to make sure that they weren't followed.

He carefully selected an appropriate size bush, slipped his pack off and stowed it underneath. Free from the cumbersome load, he pulled his small field binoculars from the pack and carefully made his way back to the roadway.

He picked out a small sedan and crouched down behind it for cover. With great caution he scanned the roadway and sidewalks, first northward and then southward. They had passed some people walking south, but no one spoke to them. They all seemed non-threatening, but that could be deceiving. Most of the people that he saw were not carrying any gear or had a small cinch sack. Some carried thin plastic grocery store bags filled with items Jake could not make out. *Not gonna get far with that*, he thinks. He spied a small family group moving south, each member carried a small backpack emblazoned with brightly colored cartoon characters, probably ones bought for the first day of school. *Hey if it works*, he thinks. The father figure was pulling an uncovered wagon loaded with supplies. Jake could see canned food, a couple of gallons of water, a tent, and a sleeping bag. *Not too smart to pull that uncovered*, he thought. *Maybe I'll try to educate them if they want.*

He turned his gaze southward again. This time he saw one person that caught his interest. A male form, hunched over, stopped in the shadows on the opposite side of the roadway. He was far enough away that Jake could not make out any discernable features. The outline suggested an overcoat and the person carried a briefcase or laptop bag. He was not moving and he was facing the park. Jake frowned. *I don't like this. Who is this guy? Is he a threat?* Before he could decide on a proper strategy, the male turned right and moved through the bushes between the sidewalk and into the nearby subdivision, away from the park. Jake waited another five minutes before finally deciding that the person wouldn't be coming back. *Now where did that family go?* He scanned up and down the street and they were no where to be found. *Good luck to you all, you're gonna need it.* One more thorough scan and he went back to meet with the women.

He found them sitting under a large pine tree, using the shelter of the huge, dense boughs. They sat on the soft bed of dry pine needles going through their gear looking for food. Their pant cuffs and outer coats were still wet from the earlier drizzle.

"Change your socks if your feet are wet, you'll thank me later." Jake said as he crouched down to join them. They nodded and pulled out a pair of dry socks from their packs. Jiang-Li crinkled up her nose as she pulled her pair out. They were men's gym socks, hopefully clean, but no one knew.

"Hey, it's better than no socks at all!" Jake said. They all agree, and fall into a relaxed silence. Janey finally broke the stillness, "What do you think happened?"

He looked to her, "to cause all of this?" as he waved his hand around.

"Yeah."

"EMP."

"EMP? What is an EMP?" Jiang-Li asked.

"ElectroMagnetic Pulse, it is generated by a nuclear blast." Jake answered. The two women grew tense.

"Nuclear blast? Where did it hit? Is there danger of fallout or radiation poisoning? Who launched it?" Their questions flew fast and furious. He held up a hand to quiet them.

"Hold on, hold on. I don't have any answers, only guesses. I think that there may have been multiple nuclear strikes on us, but the first was the EMP." He looked at them and sighed. They were scared and so was he, but he could at least tell them what he thought had happened.

"Well, I had been reading up on the state of political affairs between us and North Korea, right? Our president and their glorious leader weren't seeing eye to eye, and I think that someone finally just had enough of the other and they launched an InterContinental Ballistic Missile or ICBM, at us. I am guessing that the attack was two pronged. The first strike was an ICBM that was detonated at a high enough altitude to cause the EMP. That took out our electronic devices, computers, cars, that sort of thing. This basically disabled the civilian population and caused them to overwhelm the civil services. Police, fire, and hospitals become flooded with people. Communications and traffic flows come to a stop." He paused and scratched his nose.

"While that is all going on the second strike begins. They either hit us again with their own nukes or maybe it was our own nuclear power plants overloading. I don't know which, but I do know that I saw a bright flash and a mushroom cloud south of us." Janey's eye's flew wide and her mouth gaped.

"Mushroom cloud? Like in those old film strips we watched in school? That kind of mushroom cloud?" She couldn't believe what she was hearing.

"Yeah, but it could have been the Fermi Nuclear Power Plant down in Monroe county or it could have been Detroit getting hit. You didn't see it?" He asked the ladies.

"No, we don't have any windows in the lab areas and we moved around so much that we missed it. My God." She put hand to her mouth. He continued on.

"Well, I hope it was the plant. If it was Detroit, I think it would have been brighter and we would have felt the shockwaves. But that depends on the yield. As for the fallout or radiation, if either of those places were hit or went critical, I don't know, I am not a nuclear scientist or a meteorologist." He paused again and took a deep breath.

"Then there is the rest of the country and I'm afraid that some more ground detonated attacks could have happened." He took a long drink from his water bottle, the women hanging on every word.

"How would you know that?" Janey asked.

"I don't. It just makes sense. See, they basically shook our ant farm to disrupt us and then they are free to hit our military bases and naval fleets. They would need to do that in order to wipe the USA off of the global map." Jake paused and bit down on his protein bar. Janey stared off into space, processing the information Jake had shared with them. A series of questions started piling up in her mind.

"If the EMP caused all of this chaos that we are dealing with now, then why hit the bases? Aren't they without power too?" Jake shook his head.

"Not necessarily, some bases would be hardened against an EMP. Especially the missile bases and radar installations. If the military had enough lead time then I would wager that our glorious leaders are now in some bunker underground and I would bet that the midwest is a radiated wasteland." He took another bite of the protein bar.

"Let's get back to the nuclear bombs. Don't they expel radiation when detonated? So you mean fallout?" Being chemists and working in a lab, they were familiar with radiation. They had become agitated at the thought of the byproduct of nuclear doom that they couldn't see, smell or touch.

"Yep, fallout. We might get some, we might not. It depends on the yield of the weapon and how close it was detonated. Ladies, calm down. We are speculating about something that we have no evidence of. Right now, we need to focus on getting the kids and then going home."

"But what about the fallout from the first ICBM? You said it was detonated at high altitude, right? So couldn't the high winds in the upper atmosphere bring it to us?" Janey was almost shaking. He took her into his arms and held her tight.

"No, the fallout from that detonation will dissipate and disperse over a much larger area and will not be a problem for us. In fact it won't be much more dangerous than getting an x-ray at a hospital. Then let's consider that maybe other sites out west were hit, then we run the risk of fallout from those blasts. It all depends on the weather and how far the wind blows it. In fact, I think that the storm that just moved through was a higher power protecting us from whatever happened south of here. Sort of like washing the world clean?"

He was trying to be reassuring, not just for her and Jiang-Li, but for himself as well. He had researched how to protect himself and his family from nuclear fallout. All of the plans he had found said to build an underground shelter and that was out of the question where they lived.

"So when is it going to be fixed? You know, like when will we have power again?" Janey sniffed and wiped her eyes.

"I don't know. Probably not for a very, very long time. Imagine living in the 1800's again. Like Little House on the Prarie times."

"Do you think the United States launched any ICBMs at North Korea?" Jiang-Li asked. Jake noticed that her eyes were wide with great fear and anxiety. Her chest was heaving quickly and her hands were trembling.

"I would think so, yes. Them and probably any allies they had. Why?"

"An EMP? Like here?" Her anxiety grew worse. He looked to Janey for help or guidance. She met his gaze and shrugged. He turned back to Jiang-Li.

"No, I think that if we launched anything it wasn't to take out their electric grid, it would be to cause utter and total nuclear devastation," he answered grimly. "Mutally assured destruction."

"What!?!?" Jiang-Li stood up and started speaking in Chinese, her voice rose in pitch and volume.

She cried out hysterically in a language neither of them spoke. She flung herself to the ground and began sobbing uncontrollably. Janey pulled away from her husband and went to comfort Jiang-Li. She held her tenderly and gently rocked her back and forth.

"What's wrong Jiang-Li? Please tell me. You know we can't speak Chinese. Shhh. It's okay." She glared at her husband, and silently chastised him for what he said. He mouthed one word back: *Sorry*.

Together they sat quietly, while Jiang-Li tried to get control of herself. Janey glared at Jake, while he got up and checked to make sure no one had heard the outburst. Pulling back from Janey's grasp, she sniffed and wiped the tears from her eyes.

"I am so sorry for that." She was clearly embarassed about her emotions.

"It's ok, Jiang-Li." Janey smiled at her. "What were you saying? If you don't want to tell us, that's ok. We are just curious."

"No, it is ok. I was grieving for my mother and father. My aunts and uncles. My family. They live in a little village near the border of China and North Korea. If what your husband says is true, then they must all be dead."

"How close to the border?" Janey asked.

"Actually it would be considered a suburb of Beijing." About sixty miles west of the the border."

"I don't think that they would be dead, Jiang-Li." Jake said as he stepped back under the cover of the trees.

"What? How?" she looked to him, shocked. He looked from Jiang-Li to Janey and back to Jiang-Li. *They are scientists, chemists, right? They have bachelors and masters degrees, and all I have is an associates degree, in Computer Science of all things! How could I know more than them?* He cleared his throat.

"You see, the weather patterns flow from west to east, so any fallout and radiation would be pushed out to the ocean, away from China. If anything Japan is in danger of fallout, again." He thought back to history class and the lessons on WWII.

"Are you sure?" her eyes searched for the complete confirmation of his belief. He realized that her fragile psyche hung in the balance, he nodded.

"Yes, I am sure."

"Oh thank you Mr. Jake!" Jumping to her feet she flung herself at him and enveloped him in a hug. Janey stared at them in complete shock and awe. He looked to his wife for help, but she could only laugh.

CHAPTER 21

Francis froze in his tracks. Up ahead in the distance, he had watched his prey turn off the pavement and into a small city park. Then he had seen their infernal leader, Jake, come back to the entrance. He had taken his pack off and laid it down under a bush. *What does he have in his hands?* Francis had stopped in mid stride, underneath the long, low boughs of a maple tree. The sky had become overcast and the large wide leaves of the maple shaded him from sight.

The leader of the pack held something small up to his eyes, and for a brief moment Francis could feel his gaze upon his skin. *Can he see us? He can!* The thought broke Francis from his statue like demeanor.

"Did he see me? Does he know it's me?" He whispered to the commanding voice in his head.

"Yes, I think he saw us, but I don't think he knows it IS us. If he did, he wouldn't still be lying there, right?"

"Yeah, you're right!" he said a bit louder this time. The fear and panic started to dissipate from his gut.

"Best to find some better cover, just to be sure." He nodded and took one slow step backwards. He could see the enemy's big fat head turning slowly away from him, toward a new threat. A small group of people were moving towards him, two big people and two little people. Jake's gaze seemed to be fixated on them instead of him. He stole a glance behind him and spotted a break in the bushes.

"It's a backyard, a neighborhood! GO NOW!" He broke into a trot and dove through the opening. He hit the ground hard and slid into a small pool of standing water in someone's yard.

"Great, just freaking great!" He hefted his now soaked laptop bag as he stepped out onto some drier grass.

"It's fine, the bag was sealed from the water," the voice reassured him. He felt around in his pockets worried for his other posessions. The cold heavy steel of the handgun pressed against his outer thigh. He slid his hand into the pocket and gripped the firearm. Francis was a novice when it came to firearms. He wasn't sure what he had or even how properly work it. He didn't care. All he cared about was getting even with those that wronged him and the company. His grip on the gun became painful and the metal felt white hot in his palm. He could taste the anger in him rising like bile.

"Not yet," the voice pleaded but Francis ignored it. He carefully inched closer to the opening he had come through and searched for those probing eyes. His gaze darted back and forth looking for the leader. He was gone!

"Where did he go? We must find him!" The voice pitched higher in despair.

"No, not yet. We will find him. It's good that he didn't see me, but he will. He will look at me and know that I am not a coward and weakling and that I can hold my own in this New World, as he put it!" The thought of getting back at those that had wronged him blinded him to the advance of a small family.

"Hey buddy, you ok?" The male said.

"Daddy, he doesn't look so good." A small voice said from behind the female.

"Yeah, honey, maybe we should leave him be." The adult female clutched at her companions arm.

"No, we need to help our fellow man." He turned back to Francis.

"Is there anything you need? Maybe we can help? We don't have much." The sudden voices startled Francis from his revenge filled thoughts. He pulled the gun from his pocket, the hammer caught on the fabric and he almost dropped it.

"How dare they question us! Don't they realize that they will let him know where we are? Kill them, NOW!"

Francis fought for control over the voice. He smacked his head with one hand while the other still held the gun. The cold metal and sharp edges scratched deep furrows in his scalp. He turned on the family.

"No. I do not need your help! What I need is for you and your spawn to leave! NOW!" he spat at them. They had all backed up at the sudden sight of the gun. The children whimpered in fright. The man held his hands up.

"Hey, hey, hey, man! Hold on now! We were just trying to help. We mean you no harm!"

"Please don't hurt us or the children!" The female pleaded. Francis's gaze fell to the children and the gun wavered ever so slightly, then the grip became firm again.

"I just want to be left alone!" He pointed the metal device capable of inflicting death and destruction, at the man's head and pulled the trigger. *CLICK! He blinked twice in confusion. The gun didn't fire. Francis stood his ground and looked at the firearm then the family. They should be dead by now.

"Why didn't it fire, what did you do wrong Francis? They are not dead and it is all your fault!" The voice admonished him.

"No, it is not my fault, it's this stupid gun's fault!" Francis ranted while the family stared at him.

The man motioned for his wife and kids to run, he mouthed the word *GO* to them and waved them on.

"Listen pal, we don't want any trouble, ok?" He began to move past Francis, but he wasn't listening to the man. The man saw that his eyes were wide and tears fell down his cheeks.

"You know I don't know how to use guns, I've only ever seen them in video games! I don't care what you say, it wasn't my fault!" Francis continued to rant.

"Fine, maybe the safety is on, let me check." He turned the gun over and over in his hands until he found the cause of his inability to fire the weapon. He found the small lever that turned the hunk of metal into a killing machine. He moved the lever until a small red dot appeared. Satisfied that he now could complete his mission, he looked up. He looked up and expected the family to still be there, waiting for death but they were gone. He turned round and round, but they had vanished. He chuckled to himself and made a mental note to turn the safety off first, next time.

CHAPTER 22

Jake kept checking his watch, silently marking the time until it was time to go. He also kept checking their surroundings. He couldn't shake the feeling that they were being watched. It wasn't a good feeling, he decided. He checked his watch one last time, then stood up and stretched out the kinks in his back and legs.

"30 minutes are up, let's go. Leave No Trace," He pointed at the trash on the ground in front them. The women grumbled and moaned in response. Janey gazed up at him, and winked.

"Yes sir, Mr. Scoutmaster Sir! " she said. He answered with a glare that told them he meant business.

"Sorry, just trying to lighten the mood, geez!" Janey said as she gently poked him in the side.

They packed up, policed their trash and moved out. Jake checked his map and after a few minutes of getting his bearings, he pointed north.

"We need to get to 19 Mile Road and Ryan for our next stop. That's four point one miles. We aren't making as good time as when I was alone. My calculations may be off from here to home. Let's do our best."   He knew they weren't making good time and he had to keep telling himself that it was ok, as long as they were together, all would be ok.

"We will be cutting through a couple of neighborhoods to shave off some time. Hopefully it will be to our advantage anyway." Shouldering their packs they continued on. They walked on in silence, gently being warmed and dried by the sun that had started to peek out from the clouds.

"Thank God!", Janey said turning her head to the sky and smiling, "Maybe we will dry out a bit!" The first two miles went by quietly and quickly. The only bit of life that they saw was the skittering of the occasional squirrel or the flittering of a small bird. The only sound was their foot falls and the rhythmic clicking of the hiking staff that Jiang-Li held. In the distance the large plumes of black smoke could still be seen when they stepped out to cross a major avenue or thoroughfare. Only once did another person cross their path. A younger man, with blond hair and a beard, carrying a pack of his own. It looked worn and well used as did the owner. Their eyes met and without a word, they knew that each had a long road ahead of them. The man nodded to each in acknowledgement and to convey he meant them no harm. They did the same back. *I hope that the rest of our interactions with any people we meet go like that and not like with Yellow Sneakers.*

Jake thought back to his earlier encounter with the street thug. Only mere hours into the blackout and some folks had already devolved back to a more primitive behavior pattern. He had tried to leave peacefully but instead he had to resort to violence to survive. *It was me or him, he just wanted my things, whereas I wanted to get home to my wife and kids. So does that mean, I am no better than him? I killed him over MY things. Should I have just let him have my possessions? He might still be alive if I did. But would I? Probably not. No, I need everything in my bag to get home safely. What would he need with a backpacking stove or thermal blanket? He only wanted my money or food, of which I have very little. No, I did the only thing I could to protect my life, my wife and ultimately my kids.* He sighed heavily, and looked to the heavens, silently asking for forgiveness and absolution. He was not sure if he would get it. He checked his watch again, *damn, still slow. It's ok, slow and steady wins the race.*

The weather had finally seemed to cooperate with the trio. The standing water had drained into the gutters and the yards and grassy areas soaked up the water quickly. The sun had done it's job and dried out their clothes and packs but it was also starting to heat up.

"Make sure you drink plenty of liquids, a hydrated scout is a happy scout, a dehydrated scout is a, well, let's not get dehydrated." Jake took out his water bottle and drank deeply. The women followed his example.

"Excuse me, please. What is a dehydrated scout?" Jiang-Li was new to the scouting experience. Jake explained to her the meaning of the phrase.

"It's what I tell my Boy Scouts when we are camping Summer or Winter, water is the most important item to bring or find when you are out in the wilderness. Dehydration is nothing to disregard. Even in the colder months you can get dehydrated just from breathing! I tell them that a hydrated scout is a happy scout and a dehydrated scout is a dead scout, and a dead scout makes me have to do paperwork! I hate paperwork," he said with a grin. Janey nodded, "He sure does!"

"Oh, ok." Finally understanding what he meant.

"Excuse me please, I have another question. I have noticed that you keep looking at your watch. I thought that the EMP would have stopped it from working. Are not all watches electronic? That is to say, they need batteries?"

"Yeah, I saw that too," Janey joined in. He sighed in exasperation and mild frustration. He looked between them and took a deep breath, calmed himself, *they are just curious and want to know.*

"Well, not all watches need batteries. Those are most commonly called quartz and this little beauty here is an automatic" he held up his wrist so she could see the watch face. The second hand slowly ticking away. TICK TICK TICK. She smiled and still looked puzzled.

"Ok, this watch doesn't need batteries or electricity to run, it works on the gear and pinion principle, with an asynchronous winder!" He smiled and chuckled to himself. Janey laughed a little as well. Jiang-Li didn't get it, she was more confused now.

"Gear and pinion? Asynchronous what?" she asked. Her answer made Jake laugh even harder.

"Excuse me, I just don't understand!"

"Jiang-Li, please forgive him, he is an ass of the highest order." Janey punched him in the bicep, not hard enough to hurt but enough to tell him to knock it off.

"He is quoting an old children's animated Christmas show from the late '70s, maybe even early '80s. It was called The Night Before Christmas and was about a family of mice that lived with a human family. Anyways, one of the mice decides to get a look at a massive town clock and asks his father what it runs on, and that is what he says, gear and pinion and asynchronous whatsit. Again, I say, he's an ass." Her look was stern but kind.

"Oh ok, I understand that now. Very funny Mr. Hawkins."

"Jiang-Li, please call me Jake. I am sorry for making fun. It just struck me at the time."

"Oh Sorry, Jake. Could you please try and explain your watch again?"

"Yes, properly this time!" Janey said with that mom tone, that only mothers had and could use at their whim.

"Alright, alright. I don't know how it all works together, but I'll tell you what I do know. Instead of a battery or other electronic device, the watch is run by using a counterweight that spins around a central pin. That spinning then winds a spring. That spring stores the energy and is used by the rest of the clockworks to keep time. It is a mechanical or automatic watch."

"I have three more like this at home. They can sit and sit, waiting for someone to pick them up, give them a shake and away they go." He took off the watch and showed her the see through back. As he moved it she could see the counterweight swaying back and forth.

"Three more? I was not aware of this?" Janey asked. She hated it when he spent money on things that she didn't know about.

"Yeah, I have a blue faced Invicta, Big Ben, and finally a Seiko with a green face and band."

"Oh yeah, ok. I forgot about those. I didn't realize they were automatic." Janey shook her head.

"Excuse me please, Jake. Big Ben?" Jiang-Li was very inquisitive about the watches, but that was ok with

Jake. It passed the time on their journey. He smiled at her as he spoke.

"Yeah, I call it Big Ben because it has roman numerals on it instead of the normal numbers. It reminds me of a grandfather clock or Big Ben in London."

"Were these watches part of your preps?" Janey was finally coming around and seeing all of the little things that Jake had been accumulating over the years. Almost like he knew something of this magnitude was going to happen.

"Not at first. Initially I really liked the look and was going for a James Bond Omega Seamaster look. That was back before I started getting involved with prepping. But once I did, yeah, the last 2 were. I also have another Seiko sitting in a box in the closet for Joey." Their conversation fell silent as they approached their next rest stop area.

The intersection was littered with cars, some were smashed with the occupants still inside. Others were clearly abandoned, doors standing wide open. Jake peered inside the empty ones, scanning for anything of use or value. He spotted a few sealed bottles of water in the back seat of a nearby truck. He lifted the door handle and was surprised to feel the lock release and the door open.

"Hey, check some of the abandoned cars for water or food!" He turned back to the bottles he found, scooped them up and slammed the door. He stowed them in his pack and moved to the next car. Just as he peered in the window he heard a distant rumble. *Thunder?* He looked up and only saw clear sky above. The distant rumble was getting louder and closer. *That's an engine! Someone is coming!*

"HIDE! NOW!"

CHAPTER 23

Francis sat underneath the low hanging branches of the hemlock tree. It was one of many that lined the neighborhood. Time had lost all meaning to Francis, it seemed to slow down, and speed up erratically. What was only a few minutes felt like an eternity to Francis. He had to fight the urge to give up and break cover to see if his prey were still in the park.

"NO! Stay put!" Always, the voice knew what to do and when.

"Ok, but just a few minutes more." He was talking to himself more and more. It didn't even strike him as odd that he was doing it. The cold metal of the gun was pressing against his leg, tucked safely back in his trouser pocket. The thin wet fabric working its best to transfer the heat to the air. He slid it out and held it up, clicked the safety and aimed carefully at a point in the distance. He imagined pulling the trigger and firing a white hot piece of metal through Jake's head.

"Bang! Bang! Bang!" He chuckled gleefully. He was so lost in his fantasizing that he almost didn't see the group leaving the park.

"SHIT! They are leaving!" He stuffed the gun back into his pocket, and hurried after them. He moved from one shadow to the next, trying to catch up. The small group of people moved further away, unaware of the danger that followed.

They moved steadily onward, ducking down behind cars and trucks when danger crossed their path or passed by. What they failed to notice, was the danger creeping up from behind. A danger that was determined. Determined and deadly.

Francis followed at a distance that kept him hidden and out of earshot. Only once did he get close enough for them to hear his footfalls. He had been fantasizing again and had stepped on a small twig on the sidewalk. It had snapped and the sound carried louder than a crack from bullwhip. The sound snapped Francis out of his reverie and he dove behind the trunk of a large oak tree.

"Stop! Get down!" Jake hissed, his head swiveling back and forth trying to locate the source of the sound. The clouds parted and a column of sunlight illuminated the broken twig on the ground like a spotlight from heaven. Almost like some higher power was trying to give Francis away. He held his breath, hoping and praying that they would continue on. He slowly peeked around the large tree, careful to stay in the shadows. The pool of light still shone on the tattletale stick.

"Great, sound and light are now traitors to us. We must be more watchful of where we step and more careful of how loud we are! Thank God that the asshat doesn't see us." Up ahead Jake was still scanning the area, the women were squatting low against a pickup truck. All eyes were on the twig. The clouds moved across the sky and blotted out the sun once more, *maybe God is on OUR side,* he thought.

"We are on the path of righteousness and we are here to settle the right and wrongs of this Earth! It is up to us to punish those that break the law and order of man!" The voice proclaimed.

"Yes, we are!" He stayed hidden until he could no longer hear their footsteps or voices. He waited a few minutes more, then looked out again. They had made it to the intersection and were turning to go east.

He followed along, carefully waiting until they had turned a corner before moving ahead.

"We are Gods' warrior, a crusader for light! We are a force for Right and Justice! Nothing can stop us if He is with us!"

"Yeah, a Light Warrior!" Francis wasn't a deeply religious man. His parents had raised him in the catholic faith, and his wedding was held in a church, but only his wife and kids attended regularly. He had felt that his time was better spent at home, following up on office emails or double checking the laboratory data.

"Those dolts can't do anything right, if it wasn't for us that lab wouldn't be worth a spit in a toilet!"

"Yes, a spit in a toilet," he snickered. He was so lost in thought, that for the second time he was almost was discovered. But this time it wasn't by the pack of dogs he was tracking, but by an unknown group.

He had moved to within two hundred yards behind the dogs when an old, beat up pickup truck sped past him. He hadn't even heard it, but he knew that the pack wouldn't have missed the sound. He dove into a nearby ditch and tried to make himself as small as possible. *Please Lord make a shadow in this gully, too small to see but big enough for me,* he thought.

CHAPTER 24

Shit. This can't be good. "GET DOWN! HIDE!" Jake yelled, as he pointed to the sound of the noise. A dark brown 1970's era Chevrolet pick up truck was barreling down the road, weaving in between the stopped vehicles. The truck bounced up and over a curb onto the sidewalk and then back to the street again.

"Hey! HEY!! Over here!" Jiang-Li started waving her arms and shouting to the oncoming truck.

"PUT YOUR ARMS DOWN AND GET TO COVER!" Jake yelled at her. Janey was confused. *Why would Jake want us to get down? Clearly this person has a working mode of transportation, surely they would be willing to give a fellow human being some assistance.*

"This guy might help us, Jake. We should try to get him to stop. Maybe we have something to trade for a ride?" Janey and Jiang-Li were protesting Jake's commands much to his frustrations. *Don't they realize that people aren't exactly people anymore? When will they get it through their thick skulls that he knew what the best course of action was?* He took cover and was preparing to make his case when the truck veered off the sidewalk again.

This time it didn't appear to be to avoiding any obstacle or hazard.

Across the street another group of travellers, numbering a few more than Jake's group, were waving and hollering at the truck. Their motions were more frantic and visible than Jiang-Li's had been. They really wanted that vehicle to stop, so much so in fact that they were standing in its path. They thought that the driver would have to stop if they blocked his path. They were wrong. The engine roared as the driver pressed his foot to the floor.

It wasn't until the second and third bodies went flying into the air, that the women realized that Jake was right. Again. The group of travellers scrambled for safety, as the truck finally braked. The driver peered through the rear window and threw the gears into reverse. Again, the engine roared and the truck lurched towards the injured innocents. Janey, Jake and Jiang-Li could only watch in horror as the madman ran down the poor people lying on the ground. Their screams were cut short by the great brown metal beast as it trampled over them.

Satisfied that there were no survivors, the truck sped off, past the small group of huddled people cowering in fear. They watched it go eastward down the highway until it vanished in the immense traffic jam.

Jake and the women had hidden behind a small minivan, terrified of being the next target for the deranged driver. They stayed there until they could no longer hear the roaring of the murderous trucks' engine.

"How? How is that possible?" Jiang-Li asked, pointing in the direction of the terrible vehicle. Jake stood and brushed himself off, shouldered his pack and hefted his stick. He looked over at the wounded and dead bodies. The few survivors had come out of the ditches and hidey holes and were now tending to their fallen friends. One of the people, a man, looked up at Jake, but didn't say anything. He only shook his head and cried. Jake didn't offer any help, not that there was much to give.

"What do you mean, Jiang-Li? How what, was possible? How a person could just kill others like that?" Janey had followed Jake's lead and was ready to move on as well.

"No. I understand that man is capable of horrible acts against other men or even the earth. I am asking about the truck. I thought the EMP would have made it not work." She was directing her statement at Jake.

"Well, here's what I think. An EMP will overload the circuitry of most vehicles. That truck looked like it was made sometime in the 1970's. I think it was able to run because it does not need a computer to do so. Understand?"

"Yes," she nodded. "And no."

"See Jiang-Li, anything with a circuit board, like an onboard computer in a vehicle or a radio that was also connected to a power source, like a car battery or plugged into a wall outlet would be overloaded the second the EMP wave hit it. All of our cars and trucks today have hundreds of little sensors stuck all over the place. Some check the exhaust to make sure that we aren't contributing to the depletion of the ozone layer and other such horse shit!" He pulled a bright red handkerchief from his back pocket and wiped the sweat from his brow. He took a breath and continued explaining.

"If that truck was stored in a barn or a garage with a dead battery or even the battery disconnected, then it would not have been damaged by the EMP. Got it?" He smiled at her.

"So all we need is a car that has no battery in it, find a good battery and then we go?" Jiang-Li was trying to follow his line of reasoning. *It seems I have missed some information,* he thought.

"Well, no. Please understand that vehicles made since the early 1980's had computers first put into them. Most, if not all, computers have some form of onboard battery backup or capacitors. When the EMP hit, it would have overloaded those circuits still connected to the batteries. So not just any vehicle with a charged battery will work. Only vehicles made before the 1980's will work. Maybe."

"What do you mean, maybe?" Janey had joined in.

"Well this is, well, was, all theoretical. Back when the militaries of the world were doing their nuclear testing, they were only testing to see how much damage and destruction was done by the blast itself and didn't much care if it only affected the transportation systems. All of the reading and research that I have done pointed to an EMP taking out more than just our telecommunications and power grid. What we are talking about has been discussed by many other like minded individuals. Individuals that the mainstream media and most of America had called crack pots and doomsayers. I'm talking about preppers." They both stared at him, finally convinced that he was their best hope for survival.

"I am so sorry, Mr. Jake." Jiang-Li's cheeks flushed as cast her eyes down in shame.

"For what, Jiang-Li?"

"For drawing unwanted attention to our group. You said to get down and hide and I disobeyed. I tried to get his attention. I have disgraced myself and my family." She bowed deeply at the waist. He stepped towards Jiang-Li and gently touched her shoulder.

"Jiang-Li, it's ok. I forgive you." He smiled at Janey. She rolled her eyes and shook her head. Jiang-Li slowly stood upright, and wiped her eyes. He smiled at her, and she felt that it seemed to wash the guilt away. At least some of it. He picked up Jiang-Li's bag and handed it to her.

"We need to be more careful. We will not be resting here. We must assume that everyone is trying to take what we have. Let's go. We will keep going until we reach highway M-89. From there we turn east again and then home!" Playtime was over, he meant business. They nodded, shouldered their packs and moved on.

The road ahead of them seemed a bit more scary now, but it wouldn't stop Jake and Janey from getting home to their kids. He instructed Janey to lead for the next few miles, then Jiang-Li to follow behind her. He kept looking over his shoulder, back the way they had come.

"What do you see? Is something wrong?", Janey asked. A dark form darted out from the shadow of a large semi-trailer and disappeared behind a panel truck. *Great, we have a flea. No, that's not right. A tick. Yeah, a rotten little parasite. Kinda looks like the figure from outside the park*, he thought.

"Yeah. No. Well, I don't know. My gut is telling me that something just isn't right." He debated telling the women about the mysterious person following them. *Nah, that would just worry them more.*

"No shit, something isn't right! None of this is right! We are walking home in the middle of World War Three!" Janey blurted. Taken aback at her outburst he stared at her, his eyebrows raised in surprise. Suddenly they burst out laughing at themselves. Jiang-Li stared at them in complete confusion, shook her head and mumbled something that sounded a lot like crazy Americans.

"Do you know what Albert Einstein said about World War Three?" he asked.

"War sucks?" Janey offered, with a smile.

"Nope."

"The only way to win a war is to not have one?" Jiang-Li said.

"No, but that sounds like it came from that old eighties movie, Wargames!" They walked in silence for a few moments. Jake realized that they did not know the famous quote.

"He said, "I do not know with what weapons World War Three will be fought, but World War Four will be fought with sticks and stones."

CHAPTER 25

The rusted brown truck flew by Francis as he watched it aim for a group of people. His heart leapt at the thought that this could be the end of all his troubles. He giggled with glee when the first body flew through the air and the screams reached his ears.

"Could this be a messenger of glad tidings for us? Did he get them? We HAVE to know!" He was unsure of the answer. The screams and wails filled the air while many other people scampered away from harm. The thought of his prey broken and dead on the street was almost exciting. It was utter chaos and Francis suddenly felt his manhood was engorged. This had never happened before. He looked down at his crotch and was startled to see the front of his trousers were clearly bulging and now felt incredibly tight.

"You liked that, didn't you? You ARE a sick fuck!" The voice teased him.

"No! I mean, yes. I don't know! I never have before! I don't know what is happening to me?" He was struggling to understand what was causing him to be aroused. Thoughts of his wife flashed through his mind.

He thought of her golden hair draped across a pillow and her dark eyes fixed on his. Her smile and full breasts usually were all it took to get aroused. She spoke softly to him, beckoning him to join her.

"Francis, come to me. Come be with me." He smiled and reached out for her hand but grasped only air. Her smile changed to a frown, and her voice changed.

"Francis, you let them get away. You are not the man I married. You might as well not be a man at all!"

"No! Maggie! My darling! I didn't let them get away! They are dead now! That truck killed them for us! I can come home now!" he pleaded.

"No, Francis. Look for yourself," she pointed toward the truck, now almost a faint dot zipping between obstacles. His eyes darted to and fro, straining to see what she wanted him to see.

"There, behind the cars, Francis! You have failed me! You have failed us! They live!"

He was so lost in his hallucination that he didn't see Jiang-Li and Janey waving at the truck moments before it hit the group of anonymous travellers or hear Jake yelling at them to get down and hide.

"They live," she said. *"You failed us, Francis."*

"Us? What do you mean us?" The form of his wife stepped aside to reveal his two daughters, Janice and Brenda, only eight and six years old. They looked up at him with disappointment filling their bright, young eyes.

"You don't love us anymore, papa. If you love us, you will do this." They turned away from him vanished.

"No! This can't be! I saw their bodies crushed and mangled under the tires!"

"It is true, you saw bodies, but not THEIR bodies! It was a different group, probably deserved it, too. Now get up and get them for us, Francis. Get them for me!" He could see her standing before him, draped in only a sheet, her golden hair cascading down and over her shoulders.

"No one else can do this for you Francis, only you can. You have to!" He closed his eyes tight and rubbed them hard. When he opened them she was gone. He looked up to the street sign and quickly realized that he was close to home, only four or five miles. He could just go home and leave the ragtag group to die of starvation or thirst.

"NO!"

"But Maggie, I could come home to you in a hour or so. I could hold you and the girls in my arms and forget all about this! I, I, I could just let someone else finish them off!" His cheeks were wet with tears, yet he didn't realize it. He pleaded for Maggie to answer him.

"Maggie, please! Maggie, answer me! Janice! Brenda!" The silence told him all he needed to know. *If she wants them dead, then so be it,* he thought. All thoughts of his wife and family left him. He was of one thought, and one alone.

"They. Must. DIE!" He said through gritted teeth. His mind was on his prey, he envisioned his nemesis, Jake Hawkins. He saw his own hands around Jake's neck, strangling the life from him.

He looked up and watched them get moving again. Francis followed behind, but time and again, Jake would turn and look back. Once, he thought he was seen. Francis had stepped out from behind a large semi-trailer to get a better view. It was then that Jake turned and looked back, but Francis was quicker. He leapt towards the rear of a small panel truck, effectively blocking Jake's view of him. He feared that he wouldn't see them leaving and panic flooded him for a moment. Then he remembered what Jake had done before killing that street thug. *Christ! That feels like such a long time ago, and it was only this morning!* He fell to the ground and quickly saw their feet. They were stopped and mulling about. Jake's were pointed at the trailer. He held his breath, watched, and waited for his time to move. Soon they began to move again. They had changed direction again, north it seems, towards a well populated shopping complex.

"*The Mall. More cars, more obstacles, more people. People means witnesses. We must hurry!*" The lilting voice of his wife had returned.

"Damn it," he muttered.

"Hurry, Papa, they are getting away." The voice was no longer his wife, but had changed again. It was his older daughter, Janice.

"Yes Honey, I'm going."

M-89 had once been a major thoroughfare for travellers going east and west across southeastern Michigan. It stretched all the way to Lake St. Clair, the small body of water connecting Lake Huron and Lake Erie. In some places it was eight lanes across separated by a dark green and lush boulevard. It was lined with shopping centers, restaurants and open air malls. Those places were now just attractive places for the unprepared and lawless. It would only get worse.

<u>CHAPTER 26</u>

Jiang-Li looked up at the large, bright green exit sign, it read: Van Dyke North. Jake had moved ahead of the women and was checking the way ahead. He knew that the closer they were to a more populated area, the chances of them running into dangerous people increased.

They had successfully avoided any major confrontations. A few times they were approached by folks who were also travelling a great distance to get home. They would plead for help or assistance and Jake would try to shoo them away or ignore them. Janey and Jiang-Li, however, had more sympathy. They gave each person a Clif bar or snack bar and a bottle of water and wished them well. Jake was getting more and more furious.

"You have to stop giving our food and water away!" he admonished them.

"Jake, they are people just like us, trying to get home to their families!"

"NO! They are not like us! If they were like us, they would have the things they would need! They would not be begging for our stuff!" He was trying to get them to understand the state they were in. Food and water would soon become scarce and people would kill for more. He had already witnessed it on a smaller scale. He turned back to the road ahead, and tried to determine if the way was traversable or not. He pulled the field binoculars from the side pocket of his pack. He held them up to his eyes and scanned the vehicles for any dangers or obstacles that would slow them down. He glassed the buildings, looking for any sign of a lookout or scout. His situational awareness was on high alert. Several minutes had gone by before he was satisfied that they were safe. He waved them up to his position. They repeated this series of actions at each intersection and side road. Each time it was safe to proceed.

Soon they came upon a familiar large dark brown UPS delivery truck. Jake held up his hand in a fist, the military sign for stop and get down. Janey and Jiang-Li saw the signal and did as instructed. The driver side door was slid open, while the passenger side door was closed. Clearly the driver had abandoned his deliveries for his own safety.

The clouds had come and gone all afternoon. Janey and Jake had noticed that they had been slowly darkening. She asked Jake what they should do if it started raining.

"Babe, what are thoughts on taking cover if it starts raining? The rain could be radiated by the fallout and then we would be caught in it." Jiang-Li suggested seeking shelter in a building but Jake shot that down.

"No. Not unless it was a sporting goods store, but even then, I am not taking the chance of being boxed in with no escape." Thunder rumbled softly in the distance.

"Honey, did you hear that?" Janey said softly as she gazed heavenward. He only nodded and handed Jiang-Li his hiking stick. He unlatched the chest straps and dropped his pack. He knelt down, opened one of the pouches and dug out one of the handguns. He held it in both hands in front of him, and clicked off the safety. Slowly he walked around the United Parcel Service truck, checking the doors and surrounding vehicles for people or possible traps. He had circled the truck twice and then proceeded to check inside. He leaned out and waved them in.

"Grab my gear and get in here!" He pointed to his pack on the ground near Janey. She lifted it up and for the first time felt how heavy it was. She was amazed that Jake had been carrying that load this whole time. She lugged it into the truck and dropped it on the floor. Jiang-Li leaned the stick against the side of the truck and climbed in after her friends.

Once they were all in, Jake slid the door shut. It was quiet and only early afternoon but the clouds had darkened more and threatened to rain again making it seem like evening. Their internal clocks tried to make it feel that way as well.

They had travelled far and were now ready for a break. Many of the small stores and shops they had passed along the way were being looted or had already been broken into. They had witnessed several police officers leaving a liquor store, their arms laden with bottles.

"I am amazed at how quickly people just gave up and resorted to theft!" Janey had broken the awkward silence.

"Yes, and how easy it seemed to do such bad things too!" Jiang-Li was referring to the carnage they all had witnessed only a few hours before.

"You ladies still don't get it. Let me tell you something. Right now, there are many good and innocent people out there who only know what is best for them and their families. I am sure there are many who will do things that normally are against their nature. Such as hurt or kill to protect the ones they hold dear. It isn't the right thing, but I know I would and I have."

"But Jake, what about the police or military? Won't they be able to help? Once this is all fixed, won't those bad guys be caught and put in jail?"

"Janey, they are in the same boat we are! The EMP wasn't selective in who it would take power from, and who would get to keep it! Besides there are no more jails. It is frontier justice now. The criminals in jails are on the slow boat to hell now."

"What is that supposed to mean?" He looked at his beloved bride and sighed deeply.

"It means that for most supermax prisons, or jails where there are murders, rapists, child molesters, and all other sorts of baddies, they will institute a lockdown. Effectively locking in the bad guys and then leaving them to starve to death. I would like to think that there are some institutions that would attempt to keep the inmates alive, but even their food and water supplies will run out. What happens next is anybody's guess." The statement hung in the air between them. It was a stark new reality, indeed.

"Ok, why is it that we can't even help out our fellow man? You yelled at us to stop helping those in need!"

"Yes, I did. They will need to learn to fend for themselves. If we tried to help everyone, then we would be in the same place as them, once all of our supplies ran out!"

"No we wouldn't! We have you and your knowledge to get more!" She was smiling and trying to lighten the mood, but it wasn't working.

"There is no more! There is no more of anything! Yes, I have the knowledge to get us out of this mess, but what good is that knowledge when I am dead!" He looked at them and they finally realized that he was under a lot of strain and stress, emotionally, mentally and physically. He was trying to keep them alive and safe until they reached home. That was a lot to bear for one man.

"Listen, I feel prepared to do what I need to do, to get us home, keep us safe, and live through this. I just need you to help me when I need it." They looked at him and nodded silently. The pitter-patter sound of rain could be heard falling on the roof of the truck. In no time it sounded like popcorn popping all around them.

They sat in the truck listening to the pounding rain slam against the truck. Jake was turning the handgun over in his hands, studying the weapon and it's workings. Janey had sat on the floor of the truck, removed her shoes and was rubbing her feet.

Jiang-Li started looking through the packages and boxes that lined the shelves. She lifted one and shook it like a present. A metal tinkling could be heard inside. Using her fingernail, she pressed hard on the tape that sealed the box and slit it open. She sifted through the foam packing peanuts that filled the box until she found the source of the tinkling. She looked at Janey and Jake, grinning from ear to ear as she lifted out a set of serving spoons.

"Jiang-Li, what are you doing!? Tampering with mail is a federal offense!" Janey was astounded.

"Excuse me, but Janey, since the driver is gone and this is the end of the world, why not?" She winked at her friend and smiled. They looked to Jake for guidance, he shrugged.

"Go ahead!" Janey smiled with childlike mischief and tore into one of the boxes. Jake and Jiang-Li followed suit. They found cook books, romance novels, and technical journals, Jake looked them over and decided that nothing was worth keeping. Jiang-Li opened a couple of boxes containing laptops, Janey found three tablets and Jake opened a large box that contained an old dot matrix printer. The box looked it was wrapped by a monkey and was shipped from ebay. By the time they were done, they had found alot of kids and women's clothes. None of which fit either of the women. Jake had opened a set of kitchen knives. They were not as expensive or sharp as the Cutco set he had at home, but they would do in a pinch.

While the women were having fun opening package after package like it was Christmas Day, Jake decided to settle down for a rest. He had finally felt the pressure and exhaustion pressing on him. He decided to sit in the driver's seat and take a short nap. As he plopped down he heard a heavy thump beneath him. He leaned forward and felt around under the seat. His hand touched cold metal. He grasped it firmly and slid it out of its hiding place. He held it in one hand and looked at his find. The revolver was clean and shiny, and felt good in his hand. He opened the cylinder and found it loaded with .38 Special rounds.

"Holy Shit! Well, this thing will punch a hell of a hole in anything that is on the receiving end!" He said out loud. Janey had heard him talking and turned her attention to him.

"Where did you find that!?"

"Under the seat, if you can believe it!"

"Can I use it? You have the other handguns, and I have been feeling pretty useless lately."

"You can have one of them if you want."

"No, too many moving parts, and I always have a hard time with the safety. The revolver is easy, right? Just cock the hammer and pull the trigger!" She was smirking at him. He smiled with a twinkle in his eye.

"What did I say?" she asked.

"You said cock!" He whispered.

"You are such a juvenile!" She smacked him on the head. He took it jovially.

"Well, can I have it?"

"First I want you to hold it, and see if it is too heavy for you. Aim at something outside and pull the hammer back." He slid the cylinder to the side and emptied it of all six rounds. He locked it back in and handed it to Janey. She firmly grasped the firearm in her hands. She lifted it up and sighted in on the nearest car. She lifted her right thumb and was barely able to pull the hammer back. Once it was locked back, she put her finger on the trigger.

"Hold up, never dry fire a gun. You could ruin the firing pin. Instead, hold the hammer, pull the trigger and gently lower the hammer back to the resting position." She did as was instructed and repeated the entire exercise again. Jake watched and saw that even though she struggled a bit, she was willing to help.

"Ok, but I hope you realize that you only have six shots. Unless we find more rounds somewhere."

"Thanks babe!" She smiled wide, then gave him a deep and long kiss. She turned to show Jiang-Li her newest acquisition.

Satisfied that he was protected, for the moment at least, he checked their surroundings. The women continued opening packages and created a monumental mess that a three year old would be proud of. He smiled, leaned his head back and drifted off to slumber land.

<u>CHAPTER 27</u>

This is it, he thought. *It's now or never.* Francis had followed them all day, without incident until now. He had lost them. They had been making their way north along the highway, weaving around the dead vehicles and nature called. It had a way of calling at the most unfortunate and inopportune times. He fought the urge to relive the pressure in his bladder until the last possible second. He stood behind a pickup truck, fumbled with his zipper, whipped it out and relieved himself. The sudden release of pressure felt great to him and he marvelled at how long he was peeing. It seemed to go on and on, but it finally diminished to a dribble. He tucked it back in, zipped up and looked around for his prey.

"Where did they go?" They had vanished.

"Oh no! Maggie? Janice? Help me find them!" His voice cracked as he spun about searching for the group. His pulse raced and his chest heaved. Panic had him in its tight grip.

"*STOP! Look there!*" Maggie had rematerialized before him and was pointing down the road to a big brown delivery truck.

"What? What am I looking for?" He begged.

"*The delivery truck! Look at the side door!*" His eyes fell upon the hiking stick leaning against the side of the truck. His eyes caught a flash of movement through the windshield. His heart slowed as he furrowed his brows. They were inside the truck! He stood his ground and watched them talk to each other. He wondered what they were discussing, probably about him or maybe plotting to open the mail!

"*Tampering with the mail is a federal offense.*" The voice had changed again. Their list of wrongs was growing exponentially in his addled mind. This only fueled his anger and hatred more. His heart raced again and deafened him to the coming storm. The thunder rumbled in the west, but Francis wasn't listening.

From a distance he saw them smiling, laughing, and casually destroying government property. He decided to wait and see if they came out, but the voice had other plans.

"*Get them Francis! They are trapped in there. We can sneak around the back and get the drop on them. GO NOW!*" He nodded impotently.

He slowly made his way around to the side of the truck, putting himself in a perfect position to take them

down the second they came out. It did obstruct his view
of the Alpha, but that was okay, he could see the side of
his head through the side window. *I have you now, you
fat bastard,* he thought. The rain started to fall slowly
with tiny misting droplets. His coat was quickly soaked
in wetness, but he barely registered the new sensation.

The voices inside the truck became quieter and he
noticed that the Alpha looked like he was dead. *Could it
be? How awesome is that!* He didn't have to do anything.
Wait, that can't be right. How would he have died? He
wasn't injured in any way that Francis knew. He highly
doubted one of the women killed him. If they shot him,
why didn't he hear it? He slowly and carefully crept
around the rear of the truck and saw that the back of the
truck had doors not a sliding panel like most delivery
trucks.

"*It seems fortune is smiling on us again! We are
blessed! Our crusade is righteous! You ARE the Warrior of
Light!*" He felt the encouragement from the mysterious
voice flow through him. His confidence was boosted
and he was sure that his plan would work. He would
get the drop on the women and once they were out of
the way it would just be him and the Alpha.

"*The Alpha and Omega. The perfect dichotomy!*"
He liked that. He liked that a lot. *This pack of dogs is
about to be taken to the pound,* he thought.

He reached up slowly and carefully grasped the cold, wet handle. *This is it. Don't get scared now,* he told himself.

"PAPA!" A young girls voice pierced the air. Francis froze in place, his eyes frantically scanning the surrounding area.

"Brenda?" he whispered. It had sounded exactly like his own daughter. He let go of the handle and scurried for cover behind a nearby sedan. His eyes continued to scan each car and truck, storefront and building. His rage and anger had vanished from his dark heart.

"*NO! It's not Brenda, you stoddering dolt! GO NOW! Do it!*" Demanded the voice.

"I can't, Brenda, she needs me. I have to go to her." He stood up and continued searching for his little Brenda.

"PAPA! NO!" The girl screamed again, this time Francis saw her. She was the same height as his Brenda, and she had long, black hair like her, too. Behind her was a busted storefront window, a large gaping maw of blackness and despair. The jagged glass looked like the mouth of a long dormant beast that had awoken and was on the verge of eating its first meal. Inside the mouth stood a man motioning to the little girl to come to him.

"PAPA!" Francis jumped at the sound and he saw that she was pointing at him. Somehow it wasn't at him, it was at another figure, a male figure, and he was closing fast on the truck. The little girl ran to the man in the window and was scooped up into his arms. They disappeared into the inky darkness within.

"*He wants our prize, Francis! He is going to take it from us! You must stop him!*"

"No! I can't allow that to happen. These people need to be punished for what they have done and I must be the one to do it!"

"*Yes, that's right Francis. We must punish them!*" He looked back to the little girl, and wiped the wetness from his face, the rain had mixed with his tears.

"I am sorry, Brenda, I must do this. Please don't think any less of me."

"*Oh shut up about Brenda! Hurry Up! He is almost to the truck!*" The voice was teasing him closer and closer to the edge of sanity. Anger and rage surged within him, he drew the handgun and advanced towards the truck.

"No. I will end this, once and for all!"

CHAPTER 28

BANG!

The rear doors were flung open wide and the first bullet ripped through the smily smirk on the Amazon box before the trio had a chance to react. The bullet travelled uninterrupted through the box and into the womanly form holding it. It disappeared into her chest and out her back spraying the wall behind her in bright red. She had been standing closest to the door as it swung open and had turned toward the sudden appearance of light.

BANG!

She cried out in pain as the second bullet tore through her left leg. She fell to the floor of the truck, tumbling amidst the opened boxes and packages. The other female form screamed and had started to move towards the first. The shooter took aim at the second form and pulled the trigger, click. He tried again, click. The gun had jammed or was out of ammo. No one knew which, especially the shooter.

Screaming in rage, he threw the gun at the occupants, climbed into the truck and lunged for the second woman. She screamed and shrank away from his reach.

BANG!

BANG!

BANG!

The first bullet tore through his shoulder and out his back. The second bullet punched a hole through his liver, pancreas and kidney. The last bullet passed through one of his lungs and shattered his shoulder blade. It deflected and lodged into his spine bringing splinters of bone with it to sever his spinal cord. The force fired upon him was tremendous, but he never felt it.

The shooter was spun around by the bullets perforating his torso. The last bullet launched him from the rear of the truck onto the sedan behind it. His body slid down the hood and onto the ground. His dark red blood mixed with the puddling rain and flowed into the storm drains.

The shooter mumbled something too soft to be heard, his eyes frantically spun in their sockets. He was desperately trying to find something to lock on to. When they did, they stopped on a tall, dark male form standing over him. The man knelt down and listened intently. The shooter whispered only to him, then let his head fall back. His breath coming in quick, short gasps. The man stood up and took aim.

"I'm sorry," He said.

The shooter raised his arm and everything went black.

CHAPTER 29

The sudden sound of the rear door opening startled Jake from his nap. He jumped out of the truck as the back door was flung wide. He stumbled out into the rain, slipped and fell flat on his back. His head bounced on the asphalt causing him to see stars. The shooting had stopped before he had regained his footing. He braced himself on the side of the truck to help keep him up. He worked his way to the rear of the vehicle, rubbing his head as he went. All sounds had ceased. He didn't know if the screaming had stopped or if everyone was dead or if he had gone deaf from the head trauma. He wouldn't have that answer until he rounded the rear of the truck. He drew his handgun and stepped out to confront the assailant, but he quickly saw that he was down and no longer a threat. He turned back to the truck expecting the worst.

There was blood everywhere. On the walls, the floor, and all over the packages and boxes.

"Jake! Oh my God, Jake! Help me! What do I do?" Janey was holding her jacket to Jiang-Li's chest to try and stem the flow of blood. They both knew that you couldn't put pressure on a chest wound. That would make it worse for the patient. He noticed that her leg was bleeding as well. It appeared to ebb and flow with her heart beat. *This isn't good,* he thought.

"I, I, I don't know," he stammered. He had never trained for trauma wounds before. Even with his Boy Scout training he only knew some basic first aid.

"Janey! Are you hurt? Did you get shot?" he needed to know her status.

"I don't know, and right now I don't care. Help me save her!" All she knew was that Jiang-Li needed help, badly. Jiang-Li had started speaking softly in her native tongue. She took in a labored breath and looked up at her friends. She smiled at Jake and Janey as blood leaked out from the corners of her mouth.

"Thank you for being my friends. I wish you happiness and long life. I go now to be with my family." Her eyes slowly unfocused and her gaze shifted. She looked past them, into the beyond. She could see her husband or some long ago ancestor was calling to her. Her breathing slowed more and then finally stopped. Her body sagged in their arms. She was gone.

"Jiang-Li! Come on, stay with me! Jiang-Li! Breathe for me, JIANG-LI!" Janey was shaking her friend, trying to bring her back. Janey cleared an area to lay her friend flat. She knelt over her and started chest compressions.

"Come on, help me Jake!" He stared at her with tears in his eyes.

"She's gone, Janey. Let her go."

"NO! She's not gone! No!"

"It's ok, honey. Let her go to be with her family. It's what she would have wanted." He put his hand on her shoulder and she slowly stopped the compressions. She turned to him and he held his wife tight as they both wept openly.

They sat holding each other for what seemed like forever, and to them it was. After a few moments, Jake pulled back and looked at his wife.

"Are you hit? Did you get shot?" She felt around herself, and was relieved to be spared.

"No, my heart is racing and my hands are shaking, but I think I'm ok." She sniffled and wiped her eyes.

"Good."

"Who was that? Why did he shoot at us? What did he want with us?" Her questions were coming fast and furiously. He did not have the answers for her.

"Did you return fire?" He thought back to the quick training with the revolver."

"No, I thought you did." They looked at each other, without speaking they knew what the other was thinking: *Who shot the shooter?*

They slowly rose from beside their fallen friend and pushed towards the rear of the truck. Jake looked around for another shooter. The rain had made it difficult to see very far. He didn't see anyone close by, but that didn't mean that they had run off. Jake stepped down and turned back to help Janey. A dark form stepped out from the side of the truck.

"Francis!" Janey gasped. Jake spun around and drew his handgun. *The dark form that had been following us was Francis all along,* Jake thought. Francis didn't seem to acknowledge them, but they could see that he held a gun.

Francis stood in front of them, tears streamed down his face, his arms hung limply at his sides, the gun firmly grasped. Janey started to climb out of the truck.

"Move slowly and don't take your eyes off him," Jake cautioned as he aimed at her former boss. She moved slowly and deliberately, watching Francis the whole time. He was holding his head and openly crying while pacing back and forth.

"What did I do? What did I do? I killed that man! I know he would have taken my prize, I know that, but why?" He kept repeating himself over and over. Jake looked at Janey, she could only shrug. This was something that neither one had ever encountered before. Francis smashed the gun against his head, drawing blood.

"I know they deserve to join him, but I can't do it. I just can't!"

"Who is he talking to?" Jake asked sharply. She could only shake her head. She motioned for Jake to lower his gun. He pretended that he didn't see it. Francis stopped his pacing and looked at them. His hands were shaking badly.

"Francis?" Janey called his name softly.

"Can you talk to me? It's Janey, Janey Hawkins."

"I KNOW WHO YOU ARE! I KNOW WHO BOTH ARE!" He roared at them. Jake's grip on his own handgun tightened. He quickly looked around for some safe cover, away from Janey.

"Okay, okay, please Francis, put the gun down." Janey had put her hands up, palms out and was still trying to get through to him. He had turned away and started pacing again.

"No, you don't control me anymore. No, you don't own me. You are not my wife. She loves me and wouldn't ask that of me." *He is out of his freaking mind!* Jake thought. He looked at Janey with eyes wide, then tilted his head to the left indicating something. She looked around and understood. Jake took one step away from Francis, but he was stopped.

"Don't you move, you DOG!" Francis spat at Jake.

"You are a worthless dog! A cur! YOU should be put down!" Francis snarled at him. He raised the gun and aimed for Jake.

"Francis! Would Maggie want you to do this? What about Janice? Or Brenda?" The final name struck Francis hard. He looked at Janey and his eyes filled with tears.

"Brenda? No. She is my flower, my baby girl, my everything. No, she wouldn't want me to do this. She would want me to come home. I miss them so much, but you stole from the company! I am in charge and I am going to be in trouble for what you did! I might even get fired because of you. I, I, I just don't know what to do!" he stammered.

"Francis, listen…" Jake started.

"NO! YOU DON'T GET TO TALK TO ME!" he thundered.

"Janey, a little help?" Jake pleaded.

"SHUT UP!" The gun had come up again.

"You are the reason for all of this," Francis waved his hands all around.

"Jake, I will handle this. Francis, please put the gun down, lets talk about Brenda." Jake narrowed his eyes and nodded. As Janey spoke more to Francis he would smack his head with a fist or the gun. Suddenly, he yanked on his own hair and screamed at the top of his lungs.

"NOOOOOOOOooooooooo! WHY WON'T YOU JUST SHUT UP! This is all your fault! Not mine!" Jake looked to Janey, they saw that Francis was no longer speaking to them.

"Come on, Francis, put the gun down. Let's talk through this."

"He's not listening anymore," Jake hissed. Janey glared at him, and kept trying to reach Francis. He was pacing back and forth between the truck and some imaginary point that only Francis could see.

"Francis? Maggie and the girls miss you, they want you to come home to them. Forget about us and just go home." His head snapped up and he stared at her.

"Home. You're right. You're finally making sense. It is time to go home." He stopped pacing, turned to Janey and smiled. Janey smiled back with relief. Jake wasn't convinced. Francis looked down at his hands, and chuckled softly. He placed the barrel of the handgun to his temple and before they could stop him, he was gone.

CHAPTER 30

Aftermath

Jake and Janey sat in silence in the backseat of an abandoned Ford Taurus. The shock of Francis's suicide still fresh in their minds. They had never witnessed something so awful and gruesome as a person taking their own life. They had been present at the bedside of many family members when they had passed, but that was peaceful and quiet. This was loud and violent.

Jake was the first to emerge from the stunned silence. He swallowed hard and took several deep breaths. He looked at Janey and knew that she was taking this exceptionally hard. Her co-worker and boss had been gunned down right in front of her. Her hands were trembling and covered in dried blood. He gently took them in his and caressed them softly. She barely registered the movement and sensation. Outside the rain continued to fall, the darker and more turbulent clouds had missed them to the south. He cleared his throat and the sound echoed like a dog barking in the quiet interior of the car.

"Well, at least it doesn't stink in here. Seems pretty nice too," he remarked. He had always tried to diffuse tense situations with humor. It wasn't working. The shaking in her hands had moved up to her arms and down to her legs. He was afraid that she might go into shock. *Who am I kidding, she is already in shock,* he thought.

"Janey? Honey? Can you hear me?" He stroked her hands and cheek. She turned her face to his and when their their eyes met, he smiled. *Maybe she isn't in shock,* he thought. Great sobs escaped her, as she crumpled into his arms. He could only continue his feeble attempts at comforting her.

"Shhh. It's okay, it's okay. We are okay." She cried harder now, the tears flowing freely. She cried for Jiang-Li, she cried for the kids, she cried for herself, she cried for Jake. She thought of her former boss and as much as she hated Francis she didn't want this ending for him.

They sat in the deserted car, holding each other, and silently worked through the trauma they had just witnessed. They sat that way for an hour or more until finally Janey pulled away, wiped her eyes and sniffled. She looked at him and smiled weakly.

"I probably have racoon eyes, right?"

"You do, but that's okay. I'll still love you." He smiled. She smiled back, leaned closer and kissed him tenderly on the lips.

"Feeling better?" He asked tentatively. He knew better than to push her to act before she was ready.

"A little. We should do something for them." She gazed out the window at the three bodies. Francis was laying in a heap on the ground outside the UPS truck, while Jiang-Li was still on the deck inside. The shooter's body lay at the front of the vehicle they were in.

"For who? Francis? I suppose we could do something for Jiang-Li, but.." Her steely gaze stopped him cold. He knew better than to step over that line. Only once did he dare take that path and it turned into the biggest argument the couple had ever had, almost leading to divorce. He had decided then it was better to submit to her than fight. *Happy wife, happy life, right?* But now time was against them. *We still have a long distance to travel and burying bodies is the last thing I want to do*, he thought. He turned to her, ready to argue, but he stopped. He could see the pleading in her eyes.

"If we don't do this, we are no better than the worst of the worst out there. Please, Jake?"

"Ok." In the back of his mind he could hear the tick tock of a clock and every minute he spent burying a guy that put his wife through a mental hell and a woman he barely knew, was a minute that kept him from their kids.

"Stay here. I need to search out something to use to carry them, and someplace to put them."

"Find someplace nice, please." Again, the puppy dog eyes.

"Here, take this." He handed her one of the handguns he had taken from the street thugs and a spare magazine.

"It has a full magazine in it, that's nine bullets. The spare magazine also has nine in it." She began to protest, but he silenced her and showed her how to change out the magazine and chamber a fresh round. He kissed her gently and left the car.

Janey sat in the car, watching the form of her husband disappear in the lightly falling mist. She kept playing the last few hours over and over in her head. *Why did he think they had something of value? Who was he? Didn't he have family like us?* All of these questions and more filled her mind.

The rain had diminished and fallen silent causing the car to feel like a tomb. It was almost too much for her to bear. *I have to know, I HATE not knowing,* she thought. She always enjoyed mysteries, they were like puzzles to her. She couldn't leave them unsolved, usually she had solved it in the first twenty minutes of a movie or story. Jake wouldn't even play Clue with her anymore because she was so good at it.

The internal struggle finally won out and she had to at least know who he had been before society went to hell in a handbasket. She got out of the car and looked around the area for any movement. She squinted her eyes like she had seen Jake do multiple times. *I wonder why he was looking back behind us all day? Could it have been Francis? Well, I don't see anyone around here.*

"Good, all clear, now stay that way." She muttered to herself. *I'll just check his wallet, get back in the car and no one will be the wiser.* She walked to the front of the car where the man's body laid. She could see a large pool of red around him that stretched under the car. He laid on his side, his back to her. His clothes were muddy and unfamiliar. She noticed that his shoes were also filthy. *He looked like he took a swim in a sewage pond. Who was he?* She knelt down and carefully searched his pockets.

She was rifling through his possessions when Jake came back, and he asked what she was doing.

"I need to know who this guy was, Jake."

"Does it matter? He tried to kill us, but now he's gone. Let it and him, go!"

"Aha!" Triumphant at last, she held up his wallet. Jake stepped closer and put his hand in the wallet, preventing her from opening it. He looked her in the eyes.

"You might not like what you find in there. Please don't do this." This time he tried the pleading, puppy dog look. *She didn't buy it, never does,* he thought. She pulled away and flipped open the brown leather wallet. There were no pictures in it, which was what Jake feared, but instead there were six, crisp one-hundred dollar bills in the fold. Janey held them up, then handed them to Jake. *Who's the thief now?* She thought, guiltily.

"Credit card, library card, another credit card, Lowe's card, aha! His drivers license! It says that his name was Michael Joseph Smith. He lives somewhere in Sterling Heights. Hmm. Well that doesn't tell us anything." She stood defeated, her arms hung limply at her sides.

"I told you, you wouldn't like it. There is nothing in this world that makes sense anymore!"

<u>CHAPTER 31</u>

"What did we have, that he wanted? It doesn't make any sense! I bet he thought the truck had food or something useful in it, kinda like we did." Janey wouldn't let it go. Jake had tried to get her to forget it, but like a dog with bone, she wasn't letting go.

"You know it's pretty fortunate that I found that work truck." He said as he lifted the tools out of the wheelbarrow. He only had to walk a few hundred yards through the congested traffic to find a pickup truck that was owned by a construction company. He had walked back to the bloody scene pushing the wheelbarrow which contained two spade shovels and a pick-axe.

"Yeah, pretty fortunate that Jiang-Li and Francis died so close to some tools that we needed to bury them." She snapped back angrily.

"Okay, bad choice of words. Sorry." He said sheepishly.

He emptied the wheelbarrow, positioned it behind the UPS truck and climbed up on to the deck. He looked down at the remains of Jiang-Li, she appeared to be sleeping. He knelt down, grasped her arm, and quickly pulled back.

"What's wrong?" Janey had been watching him.

"She's getting colder and I don't know when rigor mortis starts to set." He knew that this was going to push them back even futher. He didn't know anything about rigor, but he felt like they didn't have time to waste. He moved through the truck until he was back in the cab where he left his pack resting on the passenger seat. A few seconds later he appeared in the package area wearing a set of heavy duty work gloves.

"Jesus, what don't you have in that thing?" Janey asked, amazed at the items he was taking out of the pack.

"What don't I have? I don't have enough food or water to last us much longer than two days!" He had slid Jiang-Li's tiny frame to the edge of the deck, and jumped down. He lifted her body up and gently placed her into the wheelbarrow. They walked over to Francis's body, silently calculating how much he weighed. Jake bent down and grabbed Francis's arms. Jake tried to lift the man's torso, but the weight was too much for him. He was just about ready to give up when Janey stepped forward.

"I'll help you. These were my friends." She said through tears. He smiled at her and nodded in agreement. Together they were able to lift Francis and place him next to Jiang-Li. Jake put the shovels and pick axe on top of the remains and started to move the wheelbarrow.

"What about him? What about Michael?" Janey asked, pointing to the body of their attacker.

"Leave him. We can't bury everybody, Janey!"

"But he's in the road Jake!" Her statement really stunned Jake.

"He's in the road? Is he going to get run over?" He was incredulous, time was ticking away and they still needed to get to their children.

He was about to argue the absurdity of the statement, but he looked at his beloved wife. He knew she needed this. He threw his arms into the air and nodded. They went over to Michael's body, lifted his arms and dragged him to the side of the road and layed him on the wet, grassy embankment. Jake placed Michael's hands in the usual manner of a corpse in a casket. He stood back breathing heavily, and looked down at the still form. Janey joined him, wrapping her arms around his waist. Jake said a short prayer, the Our Father, and made the sign of the cross. Janey held her man tighter. *Jake is a good man and he will keep me safe*, she thought.

After a few moments more, the silence was broken by the popping of distant gunfire. They gathered their belongings, and Jiang-Li's gymbag. Jake tied it to the end of hiking stick like a old timey hobo pack and gave it to Janey. She slung it over her shoulder, tested the weight and placement, then nodded. Jake hefted the wheel barrow and started pushing on to find a nice place for Jiang-Li and Francis.

"Jake! Look!" She pointed at a small, brown sign that read, Historic Utica Cemetery 1 mile.

CHAPTER 32

Two large marble pillars stood to each side of the entrance to the cemetery. An old, black, wrought iron sign stretched between them. The sign simply read, Cemetery in bright white block letters.

The cemetery itself was small, only a few hundred feet across and the same distance deep. The perimeter was lined with old oak trees, their trunks so wide you couldn't wrap your arms around them.

They had made it. They had pushed the wheelbarrow the mile or so to a place of peace and rest. Jake had argued with Janey only once. But Janey was adamant.

"Jake, don't fight with me on this. I won't be able to live with myself if we don't lay them to rest. They need to be buried somewhere peaceful since they died so violently!"

"Ok, honey, ok." He was so exhausted, physically and mentally, that he couldn't argue anymore.

They walked through the silent cemetery. Normally places like this gave Janey the heebie-jeebies. Today it did not.

At the rear of the cemetery, at the top of a small rise stood the largest and most majestic oak tree they had seen. It appeared to them that the tree was standing guard over the interred. A silent sentry keeping watch over their long forgotten remains. It was here that Janey decided to place her friends. Sometimes the couple could have mini conversations with each other without even speaking. He looked at his wife and instantly knew what she wanted. He lifted one of the shovels, took a deep breath and drove the spade into the earth. They dug two graves, one for each of their fallen comrades. This took much longer to accomplish, but Janey insisted on it. Jake could only nod and say, "Yes dear." They worked diligently, stopping for water and rest only when needed. *Tick, tock, tick, tock* went the clock in Jake's mind.

"We have to stop, this is like chipping concrete." Jake said, dropping the pick-axe. Janey looked at the shallow holes, only a few feet deep, agreeing that it would have to do.

"I guess that is ok. They won't be dug up by animals, will they?"

"No, they'll be deep enough." Jake was relieved to hear that he could stop digging. Together they placed

Jiang-Li and Francis in their final resting places. Jake glanced at his watch and made a mental note of how much time had passed.

Janey sniffled and wiped her eyes, the motion drew Jake's attention.

"Do you want me to say something?" Jake asked.

"Yes, please." He nodded and cleared his throat.

"Ok, well, I didn't really know Jiang-Li very well. But, I can say that she was a mother, she was a wife and se was a daughter. She came from poverty in China to luxury in America..." he trailed off, not knowing much more. Janey continued for him.

"She was a hard worker and never complained. We used to joke about her mispronunciation of english words. I hope that Jiang-Li is happy and with her husband now. I will miss her." They stood in silence for a moment before continuing.

"Francis was a, well, Francis was a father, a husband, and a son. He could audit a spreadsheet like no one's business." Janey smacked him on the shoulder. Hard.

"Stop it!" She admonished him.

"Sorry, I don't really know what to say." He said while rubbing the sting out of his shoulder.

"Francis was a shitty manager, and sometimes a shitty human being, but I think he tried to do what he thought was best for the company. I know he was a good father and husband and I hope that Francis will now be watching over his wife and kids." She looked to Jake for guidance. He folded his hands in prayer and looked down at the two bodies in the shallow graves.

" Our Lord Jesus Christ, we commend to Almighty God, Francis Hurley and Jiang-Li Chen, and we commit their bodies to the ground: earth to earth, ashes to ashes, dust to dust. Eternal rest grant unto them, O Lord, and let perpetual light shine upon them. Amen."

They stood together in the waning light of the day, holding on to each other. They felt grateful for another breath, another few minutes with each other. Together they filled in the graves.

=================== * ===================

As night fell they had made camp in a small municipal park called Whispering Woods. It was heavily wooded and gave them good cover from any prying eyes. Jake wished he had a tent, since the trees were still dripping on them from the rain earlier in the day. They had walked six miles hand in hand and in silence.

They sat hunched over Jake's camp stove for warmth. He had made some freeze dried chicken and rice for dinner. Janey turned her nose up at it, at first.

She hated the foods that Jake always bought for his scout backpacking adventures. He finally convinced her to take a "No, Thank You" bite. Something he had learned from her Girl Scout teachings. She wrinkled her nose at him but gave in.

"Hmm. You know, it's not half bad." She said as she ate the rest of the meal. Her appetite had returned. Jake let her eat it all, knowing that he had a spare protein bar or two squirreled away. He breathed a sigh of relief.

He would be okay, now that she was showing clear signs of recovery. *Still, it could be worse,* he thought as he lifted the tarp he had tied to a couple of trees close by. The droplets were pooling, causing the tarp to sag, and he didn't want it to tear apart. He propped his staff in the center of the tarp to keep the water from pooling anymore.

"Do you think the kids are ok?" Janey asked.

"They are just fine." He said without a moments hesitation.

"How do you know?"

"Well, when the EMP happened the schools should have gone into lockdown. They would have activated their procedures for a catastrophic event. Basically, to shelter in place, and keep the kids safe and fed. That also means that only a parent or guardian is allowed to get their child or children in our case." She was amazed at the depth of his knowledge.

"You know, I asked this once, but I have to ask again. How in the hell do you know all this stuff? Seriously!" She asked. He just shook his head and shrugged.

"Well, I read the rules and regulations of the schools in the district, like any good parent of a student, didn't you?" He asked jokingly, but he knew the answer was in the negative. She stuck her tongue out at him.

"What about my mom and your mom? Do you think they are ok?" He chuckled and looked at her.

"If your mom was at home when this started, and I think she was, then she'll be ok. She has enough food and water to get by until we arrive tomorrow. As for my mom, she also has enough food, but maybe not enough water. I've been talking to her about stocking up on water bottles and jugs in case of emergency. I hope she did. Besides, if Nick is home then she will be fine."

Nick was Jakes younger brother that lived next door to their mother. He helped take care of her and the property. Jake's mother lived on three acres of mostly undeveloped land on a dead dirt road, while Janey's mother lived in a 1970's era subdivision.

"Jake, why did you get into....prepping?" She hesitated before saying that word. She knew that Jake hated it.

Ever since the National Geographic channel broadcast a show called Doomsday Preppers, it put the whole prepping community on edge. There were people that were preparing for the zombie apocalypse or the sun going supernova or the Yellowstone Supervolcano. They were prepping for events that would never happen in their lifetimes and it made them look like they were off their rockers. Janey would make fun of them, but Jake always thought it was the producers and editors that skewed the backstories of the people involved. It gave people that were actually prepping for real events a bad name. Even though it was looked down upon in the preparedness community, it was one of the catalysts for Jake to look at his own preparedness. He found that for even the simplest disasters he was woefully unprepared.

"I started after I watched that show, 'Doomsday Preppers' on TV. It was entertaining but it made me take a real long, hard look at what could happen in our area, like blizzards, tornados or power outages. It made me realize that if we were out of power for any length of time we would be up shit creek with no paddle. But more importantly I really started after the kids were born. I'm a father, a husband, a son and a Scoutmaster. It is my job to be prepared, to protect my family. That means you and the kids, your mom, and my mom." He thought back to his father's last words to him before he passed away from lung cancer, "Take care of your mother!"

His father, Leroy "Hawk" Hawkins was a great man. He loved the wild west and old west movies. When he was a young boy, he was in scouts where he learned about wilderness survival. He used to go hunting and fishing with his father and uncles every weekend. As he got older, he was often mistaken for Clint Eastwood because of his build, stature and hawk-like squint. When he became a father he taught his son's all he knew about hunting and shooting, and about being a good husband and father. Jake still regarded his father as a man among men. He even adopted the Hawk squint, that his dad used to do when they would go hunting for pheasant or rabbit.

"Some of the things that I learned about prepping are from books or scouting, but most of it is from my dad. Just being prepared. He used to quote Benjamin Franklin, "By failing to prepare, you are preparing to fail." I guess even Ben was a prepper from way back!"

"Jake, do you have a plan? I mean, a plan for after we get home?" He looked at her and smiled.

"Yes I do, but we need to take this one step at a time. First, we get to your mom's house and see to her needs. Second, we get the kids out of school, then last, we go home." He smiled at her warmly.

"We should probably try to get some sleep because we have a lot of walking to do tomorrow." He said as he turned off the stove and set it aside to cool.

She laid back and tried to get comfortable, while he spread a thin mylar survival blanket over them.

"This ground sucks, and my back is gonna hurt in the morning, you know." She said through gritted teeth.

"Yeah, yeah. I know. Mine already does." He moved close behind her and snuggled close. That always seemed to defuse her.

They laid together, listening to the drips and drops hitting the tarp above them. The events of the day wore them down and soon they fell into a deep sleep.

DAY 3

<u>CHAPTER 33</u>

The first light of dawn filtered down through the trees, creating tiny pools of light on the small forest floor. The light refracted through the droplets of dew, casting tiny rainbows all about. Jake stirred lightly, opened his eyes and gazed at Janey, still sleeping. He cast his thoughts back to when they started dating, more than two decades ago. They were so young, barely out of their teens, ready to conquer the world. Back then Janey would go on family vacations with her family. They had slept out in tents. Camping was in her blood, whether she liked it or not. Every family vacation had been in tents, or campers. Even now, Jake and Janey would take their kids, load up the truck, hitch up their own camper and head out to adventure. *Ha! Some adventure,* he thought.

The sunlight had illuminated her head, lighting her auburn hair and creating a halo effect around her. His heart swelled with love for this woman. He knew he would do anything for her, he would never let any harm come to her. The thought of anyone or anything hurting her made his blood boil. He caressed her hair, and gently kissed her on the cheek. Her eyes fluttered and slowly opened. She squinted against the bright sunlight.

"Hi." She smiled.

"Hi." He smiled back, "How did you sleep ?"

"Not too bad, you?"

"Well I could complain, but who would listen?"

"You got that right!" She sat up and stretched her arms and back, Jake did the same. He reached over and scratched her back, she smiled and leaned into it like a cat. She sighed contentedly when he stopped. She flopped over and gave him a tender kiss.

"Thanks, I needed that."

"I know," he smiled. Their lips met again and he held her tight for a few moments, trying to block out all they had experienced so far. They broke apart and Jake pulled back the mylar blanket.

"We should get moving as soon as we can, but first, breakfast!" He held up a dehydrated food pouch of bacon and eggs and smiled a wide toothy grin. She rolled her eyes at him and snorted with disgust. She wasn't a fan of those backpacking type meals, but beggars can't be choosers.

"Fine, more for me." He had already had the small stove lit and the water was starting to bubble. Soon the food was ready, and they ate in silence. Jake kept staring off to the south. The billowing black clouds of Detroit could still be seen rising above the trees and high into the sky. The gunfire had stopped sometime in the night but the destructive evidence of the past violence still remained. Neither one felt any desire to talk about what they saw. Instead they cleaned their utensils and packed their gear, preparing to finish their journey. Jake finally broke the silence.

"We should make it your Mom's in about four hours, hopefully."

"Why hopefully?" she asked as she folded the shiny mylar blanket.

"Well, we don't really know what is between us and her. Could be more marauders or psychos or no one at all."

"Let's hope for no one at all." Janey slung her pack over her shoulder and stood up.

"Somehow I don't think we're that lucky."

"Let's make our own luck." She smiled at him and took his hand in hers.

"Together?" She stared at him, full of energy. He gazed into her eyes, bright and shining in the morning sun. He gripped her hand just a little bit tighter and nodded.

"Together."

The next few hours passed quietly and uneventfully mostly because it was still so early and because they had made it out past the really heavily populated areas . Morgan Hills and Sterling Heights were full of subdivisions, shopping malls and industrial parks.

The suburban neighborhoods of Carter Township and Chesterfield had experienced a rise in population density in the past few decades or so, but those families still had to travel a good distance for employment. The result of urban sprawl . The houses were packed in close, but it seemed that they were now mostly dark and vacant. *Maybe some of these houses are empty and they have supplies ready to be used? Water, food, camping or hiking gear? Guns and ammo? What would Janey say to that?* He looked over her, mulling over a possible decision. He was tempted to test his theory, but decided against it when he started hearing voices and dogs barking in the houses close to the road. *Best not to tempt fate and get shot, or bitten or worse.* He shook his head and moved on. *Damn.*

"Best to skirt around the super mega-mart and the building supply store, right?" Janey asked while staring ahead.

"Yeah, no need to get caught in any of that." A large plume of dark colored smoke poured out of the roof of the large department store. Shouts and screams could be heard as an enormous throng of people skurried in and out, carrying what ever they could. Tents, canned food, TV's, and radios. DVD's, towels, drugs, and yard tools. Anything and everything was fair game.

Fights were breaking out in the parking lot. People were reverting back to a more primitive state of mind. A shovel connected with skull, the body fell to the ground. The victor scooped up the supplies and ran off, the bodies of the less fortunate lay strewn about. Victims of accidents or of other humans? They did not know.

The building supply store was also abuzz with activity, it was utter pandemonium, even more so than the super mega-mart. It seemed that flames will turn some people away, but not all. Were they brave or desperate? Desperation causes even the most knowledgeable and trained person to do some stupid things. Gunshots rang out and the people scattered, seeking cover like cockroaches when a light comes on.

Jake and Janey crouched down and ran for the overpass on I-94, desparate to leave this dangerous area.

As they reached the top of the overpass, the true scope of the devastation became apparent. The super mega-mart, the building supply store, and just across the now dormant freeway, the outdoor sportsman superstore were lost. Two of the three had been or were being looted. The super mega-mart burned and the building supply store was in tatters, while the outdoor sportsman superstore still stood. Jake and Janey noticed that an armed presence was just outside it's massive oaken doors. The army of people shouting to be let in was only quieted by the repeated blasts from a shotgun toting "Security Team". Even from the distance of the overpass, Jake and Janey could tell that no one was being allowed in. What they couldn't tell was if those men were former employees or if it was the beginning of a warlords reign and the seat of his domain.

To the south they could still see the towering black plumes rising from what was left of the more urban areas of Detroit and the surrounding communities. Jake thought of his and Janey's relatives that lived just outside the city limits but still close enough to suffer from the lawlessness and criminal elements. He said a silent prayer for their safety and well-being. He hoped that they all had been away from the city when the violence started.

Below them lay another river of dead vehicles, some pulled off to the shoulder, others twisted and smashed wrecks. Some were still smouldering and most of them were empty. Janey spotted a few corpses still sitting behind the steering wheel. Forever locked in a terrible moment in time. Cars and trucks, dump trucks and sportscars, all now dormant. Probably forever. There was even a wrecked motorcycle wedged under a pickup truck. A small red puddle leaked out from under the bike and that told Jake all that he needed to know.

"Look at that." Jake pointed to the freeway.

"The only way to really travel now is on bicycle or horse, or maybe even an older model vehicle like we saw yesterday." Janey looked to where he was pointing and gasped at the sight. The freeway was well and truly jammed with traffic that would never clear.

"My God! Jake, will we ever get back to normal?" He shook his head and started walking again.

"I don't think so." He stopped and met her gaze. "C'mon, less than a mile to go" Jake reached out to her. Janey grabbed his hand, held it tight and smiled.

"Almost there," she said. She turned her head back for one last glance. *My God, what have we become?* She thought as tears blurred her vision of the death and destruction behind her.

================== * ==================

Janey's mother, Martha, lived about a mile or so from the carnage of the shopping center. She lived in a two-story house reminiscent of the 1970's. Aluminum siding built atop a solid brick first floor. The home was once full of activity. First to her own five children with her late husband John. In the late 1990's her eldest daughter Annie married, moved out and had three sons with Mark Sullivan. Then in 2000, Janey and Jake married and soon had Ella and Joey. Two of her children had outgrown the nest and were making nests of their own. By this time, her eldest son and youngest son had also moved out and were starting families of their own. The home had become an empty shell. This saddened Martha and John, but soon the grandkids were in need of daycare and the house was once again full of life and laughter. It would stay this way for eighteen years. Annie's boys had grown up and were now starting lives of their own so daycare wasn't needed for the Sullivan's. Jake and Janey's children had also passed the point of needing daycare. They were just entering their teens, but were becoming trustworthy young adults. The grandkids had grown up. Then John passed away from a sudden heart attack.

John Sickles had dealt with health issues most of his life, but he never let it slow him down. He loved everyone equally. His kids, grandkids and even those that joined his family by marriage all knew that John would do anything for them. He was an electrical engineer by trade, but he could play the piano and he used to design model trains. His death caused a deep and dark hole in the family.

The once full house was again an empty shell. Martha now lived alone, save for Kenneth, who came home on the weekends to stay with his mother and help out when needed. Martha kept herself busy during the week with odd chores and hobbies. She was quick to jump when any of her children or grandchildren needed anything. Usually, she could be found at the local Rec Center doing Jazzercise with her friends. Janey feared that this was where she had been when IT happened.

"Check it out, the mustard seed! She's home!" Janey pointed excitedly at the bright yellow Ford Focus parked in the driveway. Ella once joked that it looked like a mustard seed. Joey said it looked like it was covered in mustard, but either way, the nickname stuck. She started jogging towards her childhood home, the hobo stick bag swung wildly behind her.

Jake hurried to catch up to his wife, now banging on the front door.

"MOM!! It's us, we're here!" She knocked and peered through the windows, now darkened. No one answered.

"MOM! Are you in there?" She banged harder on the solid wooden door. A high pitched yapping was heard coming from inside.

"Maxwell! I can hear him barking!" She looked to her husband and saw him huffing and puffing his way to the porch. Jake stepped up to the door, stuck his hand deep into his jacket pocket and pulled free his keyring. He started flipping through them until he stopped on a large silver key. He grasped it tightly and slid it into the lock and twisted it. He pulled the key free and turned the handle. Janey pushed past him and swung the door open. A small white ball of fur stood before them yapping incessantly. Jake moved into the darkened house, quickly shut the door, and locked it. He shucked off his pack and set it next to the door. Janey had dropped her pack and the hiking stick to the floor. She moved through the house checking all of the rooms and hiding spaces.

"Mom! Are you here?" Jake ignored her for the moment, instead he moved with quick purpose. He drew the blinds and curtains, he locked the outer doors and windows. He made sure that the first floor was secure. Satisfied that they had not drawn any unwanted attention, he finally started to relax. He glanced at the empty, deep cushions of the couch and was drawn in. He flopped down onto it, releasing all of the past two days stress and tension. It felt like he was floating on a cloud as he closed his eyes. He would have fallen into a deep sleep right then, if not for the constant yapping still coming from Maxwell.

"SHUT UP!" he yelled. Jake loved dogs, but he hated Max. Max was one of those dogs that no matter what anyone did, he was going to do his own thing. Even if that meant humping Jake's dogs any chance he got. To make matters worse, Maxwell's owner, Kenneth, did not stop him. Maxwell was Kenneth's "Baby" and as such could do no wrong.

The sudden outburst from Jake startled the small dog enough to stop barking. He tucked his tail between his legs and shot up the steps to the second floor to the relative safety of Janey. She tolerated him a lot more than Jake did.

"Stupid Maxhole." Jake closed his eyes once more, feeling the sweet embrace of sleep taking hold.

KNOCK! KNOCK!

CHAPTER 34

Jake's eyes flew open at the suddenly foreign sound. Janey stumbled down the stairs, crying out.

"MOM?"

"Shhh!" admonished Jake. "Why would your mom knock on her own door?"

KNOCK! KNOCK! KNOCK! She knew Jake was right, but worry for her mother started to overwhelm her. She reached for the door handle, while Jake had moved to the window. He carefully pushed the curtains aside, and tried to see who was knocking on the door. A man stood on the front porch, wearing a light tan Carhart work coat with the hood up, effectively obscuring his face. He shuffled from side to side, constantly looking for something. He kept one hand in his coat pocket and the other he used to knock. Jake couldn't tell if the man was armed or not. He saw Janey reaching for the door about to let this stranger in and possibly attack them! Before he could yell, the man turned toward the window and Jake saw his face. The thick brown handlebar mustache , and horn rimmed glasses along with the short stocky stature told Jake all he needed to know.

"HELLO? I know someone is in there!" The man called out, his voice sounding muffled from inside the house.

"It's Ray! Open the door!" Jake exclaimed. Ray was the next door neighbor and someone they trusted to keep an eye on Martha. Janey yanked open the door so hard it struck the wall with a resounding thud.

"Ray!?" The sudden movement and sound scared Ray and he stepped back preparing to run. He stopped at the mention of his name. He squinted at them, trying to figure out who called his name, until he recognized Jake and Janey. She had stepped out on the porch and was peppering him with questions.

"Have you seen my mother? Why is Max here alone, and her car here? What are you doing here?" Jake pulled her back in the house, acutely aware that they were being watched. Ray followed them inside and quickly closed the door. Janey pulled free from Jake and resumed her verbal assault. Ray put up his hands and spoke.

"Calm down, calm down! First, I need you both to sit down. Then I need you to listen quietly and then I will answer any questions you may have." Jake and Janey sat down together, her heart was beating heavily and her mind was racing with nightmarish scenarios.

"Did something happen to my mom? Please you have to tell me!" Janey had been increasingly worried about her mom ever since her dad died. She was alone and in her early 70's, not old but certainly not a spring chicken. Ray looked at her and smiled.

"Yes, I have seen her, she is at my house. I was coming over to get Max and his things when we saw you two coming. With all of the craziness going on, we thought it wasn't safe to venture out!" He went on to explain that Martha had been staying with his family for last two days and they were looking after her.

"Max and Snoopy don't exactly get along and they don't eat the same food, so he has been staying here. I usually come over a few times during the day to let him out and visit. Martha came with me last night and we decided to take the dogs for a walk." He looked at them both.

"We had just made it back to the house when we heard an engine, sounded like a truck, coming down the street. Then we heard the gunfire. Turns out, it was a pickup with a bunch of numbskulls in the bed. They were throwing liquour bottles at any vehicle on the road and popping off shots at any house that had a source of light coming from it. Just a right bunch of buttholes, if I do say so myself."

"Did they see you? Are they coming back?" Janey was now worried even more for her mother's safety. Jake was eerily silent, staring off into space, but deep in thought.

"I don't think they saw us and we haven't seen them yet today. Maybe they were hung over or just passing through. Either way, Martha was too scared to leave Max here. So, my wife, Kelly, and I agreed that she could come and live with us." Janey was relieved to hear that her mother was safe, but was still aching to see her. Just then the door opened to reveal a familiar form.

"MOM!" Janey squealed and darted to her mother like a young child who hadn't seen her parent after a week of summer camp.

"Oh dear! Hi, honey, I'm okay. Not so tight!" Martha tried to pull back but Janey's grip was tight.

"Martha!" Jake stood and smiled. The sight of his wife and mother-in-law holding each other tight, filled his heart with joy. She smiled back at him.

"Oh, Jake!" She pulled him to her and Janey. Not to be outdone, Jake pulled Ray into the group hug. After a few awkward moments they finally broke apart and settled down. Martha asked about their journey and Janey looked to Jake. He cleared his throat and began his tale.

================= * =================

Once the tale had been told and the questions answered, Martha and Janey busied themselves with packing what belongings Martha would need for the foreseeable future. Ray and Jake moved to the kitchen, where they sat, taking stock of the food stuffs and packing the food up.

"What kind of preparations do you have in place, Ray?" Jake asked as he set a large can of Tomato Juice in a cardboard box that he had rescued from the garage.

"Some food and water, but only enough to last a couple weeks or so. We are good, no need to worry about us, besides, Martha already told us to take what we need from here."

"Take everything." Jake said matter of factly.

"What?"

"Take everything. If Martha is going to be with you, it would be best for you to pool your resources. Inventory it all, write down the expiration dates, create a rotating pantry. The whole shebang. I would then empty her hot water tank into some old milk jugs. Refill, reuse, and recycle. Store it in your basement if you have space. The colder the better, same with the dry goods. " Ray smiled and chuckled, shaking his head.

"What is so funny?" Jake was suddenly cross.

"Don't you think that is a little extreme, Jake? The power will be coming back on any day now, and what you are suggesting is.."

"Is what? Is what, Ray? C'mon, out with it!"

"It's a little crazy, is all I'm saying."

"It might be, and I hope I'm wrong. But what if I'm right Ray, huh? What if I am right? What then?" Ray saw how serious Jake was taking this. He thought about it for a moment and realized the truth of what Jake was saying.

"Then I guess we will be better off, won't we?"

"Yes, you will. Listen, I don't like this anymore than you, in fact, I would much prefer Martha to come with us than be a burden to you and your family." Ray cut him off before he could continue.

"Jake, you and Janey have to get to your kids. Martha isn't up to walking that distance, not with her bad knees. She told us as much already." Jake had already surmised as much from the brief encounter they had with Martha. She was stubborn and sometimes there would be no changing her mind.

"Something else to consider, Ray. It might be in your best interest to go house to house and scavenge what you can find. Take the canned goods first and don't forget the water heaters. If you find anyone still there, feel them out, see if they are in line with this type of living. Have them move closer if they can. You and Martha are situated pretty centrally on this street and there are only two entrances. Very easy to defend if needed." He could see that Ray was appalled, the open mouth was a dead giveaway. Ray stood and put his hands up.

"Hold on one minute! What you are talking about is stealing! Thievery! What if those folks are just walking home, like you and Janey? What if they come back?" Jake, not one to back down, also stood to face Ray.

"What if they don't? Ray, I need to impress upon you that the world has changed. We, as a human race, need to understand that and find our new place within it. Ray, if you don't change to survive, then I am afraid that you and Kelly and your son won't stand much of a chance." Ray was taken aback again by Jake's words and again he struck with the cold hard truth. He sat back down hard.

"This is a new world, with new rules. It is survival of the fittest. Now is the time to increase what stockpiles you have, both in consumables and knowledge. Do you have what it takes to survive, Ray?" Jake stood before him, hands folded across his chest, squinting like a hawk searching for prey. Ray stroked his long mustache, and stared at the ground, looking for answers. He knew the only answers to be found, were to be from within. He looked up at Jake. Their eyes locked. Ray looked away as shame flooded him. He thought of his wife and son, about what might happen to them if he was taken from them. He couldn't bear to imagine even the slightest of harm coming to them. He would need to be strong, and brave. He would need to be like Jake Hawkins. With new resolve and courage he stood up.

"Ok, Jake. What else should we do?"

================== * ==================

"Mom? Do you think you will be able to come with us? It is a long distance, are your knees up to this?" The women had been up in Martha's bedroom, steadily packing her clothes and personal effects for the transfer to Ray's house. Janey had been watching her mom go up and down the steps and with each cycle she was slowing. Each step now seemed like she had weights on her ankles.

"No, honey. I'm good here, with Ray. Besides I need to be here with Max and wait for Kenneth. You need to go and be with the kids. Once Kenneth gets here, then we will head over to your house, OK?" Matha answered as she gently placed a picture frame of her late husband into her suitcase. She let her fingertips caress his cheek, wishing that he was there with her.

"Mom, what if Kenneth isn't coming? It's not like we could just drive over here and get you anytime we want!" Janey was upset, and her voice was rising.

"Now, now, stop that!" Martha barked. She was one of the only people that could get Janey to calm down once she started getting hysterical, not even Jake had mastered that trick.

"I will be with Ray and Kelly. They need my help, besides, you know Jake won't let me bring Max along." She smiled warmly at her daughter.

"True, he might suggest we eat him," Janey offered.

"Or turn him into fertilizer!" They chuckled together. Max just sat at Martha's feet wagging his tail. He was excited becase they had just said his name, not because they were discussing his demise.

The thought of the house's proximity to the local Air National Guard Base worried Janey.

"Seriously though, Mom. What if the airbase is attacked? You are less than a mile away!"

"Honey, if it's time, then it's time. Don't worry about me anymore. I will be fine, you'll see. You need to stop worrying about things outside of your control!"

"But Mom…"

"But nothing. I have made up my mind. You need to stay with Jake. He will get you and the kids home safe. Then when the time is right, you can come for me. OK?"

"Ok. I don't like it, but ok." Janey embraced her mom again. She buried her face in her mom's shoulder. Martha stroked Janey's hair, and gently scratched her back. Janey arched into it, like a cat.

"Tickle back," Janey asked, her voice was muffled by her moms shirt. Martha smiled.

"Ok honey."

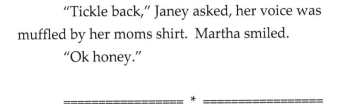

The women came down the steps with the last of the luggage as Jake and Ray carried on about gardens and how Kenneth was able to get one going in the backyard a year or so ago. Martha and Janey decided that it was time for a break.

"Ray, have you ever noticed the tall antenna on the house?" Jake asked while he pointed at the ceiling.

"Yeah, thought it was a lightning rod, why?"

"Know anything about HAM radios?"

"Not really, but I am willing to learn." Jake took a deep breath to collect his thoughts, then motioned for Ray to follow.

Upstairs in John's old study sat a computer, now just a boat anchor. Next to it was a small HAM radio.

"That? It looks like a CB radio!" Ray asked.

"Yeah, but it has better range, given the power."

"What power? In case you haven't noticed…" He gestured around in the darkened room. Jake rubbed his eyes, it had been a very trying day. He took another calming breath before continuing. He reached over to the power supply unit that the HAM radio was plugged in to. held up two leads, one black and one red, both leading to the radio.

"Positive and negative, got it?"

"Yeah, I know that, but what am I going to hook it up to?" Jake reached behind the power supply and lifted out a second set of leads, this time these had little pincer clips like affixed to the ends. They looked like little jumper cables.

"Car battery." Jake smiled.

"Could I plug it in to my generator?" Ray asked.

"Yes, but I would only use that with a charger to keep the car batteries charged."

"Ok, well, I run my gennie during the morning to keep the fridge cool."

"Good idea, I would scavenge a few car batteries from some of the derelicts out there. Have them in a cycle of charging and discharging. The radio will run off of single car battery for a few hours. I also have a HAM radio, and my call sign is KE8ITZ. Listen for me on frequency 443.550 every morning at 9am. This will be the best way to get in contact with us after this."

"How do know if it still works?"

"Let's test it!" In no time, the two men had pulled the battery from the Mustard Seed and had it hooked up to the HAM radio. Jake showed Ray how to hook up the power supply and he flipped the switch. The radio sprang to life, spewing a stream of static and causing all to cover their ears. Jake scrambled to turn the volume down.

"One of the grandkids must have messed with it." Martha said. They shook their heads in agreement. Jake tuned the desktop unit to the right frequency and set his portable HAM radio to match. He winked at Janey and went down stairs. After a few moments, they could hear his voice softly coming from the radio. Ray adjusted the volume so they could all hear.

"CQ. CQ. CQ. This is KE8ITZ. Is anyone out there? Anyone at all?" Ray lifted the receiver, and keyed the mike.

"Hello KE8ITZ, this is uh, I guess I don't have a call sign, what should I say? Over?"

"Well the FCC gives out the call signs, so I guess you could make one up? And don't say over, that's for military transmissions and 70's truckers!" Ray looked around for ideas, and one suddenly came to him.

"Hello KE8ITZ, this is KE8RAY! Is that ok?"

"KE8RAY is awesome! When you are done and ready to turn it off, just say KE8RAY clear? Ok?"

"Ok, KE8RAY clear." Ray smiled at Janey and Martha as he turned off the radio. He scribbled down the call sign on a scrap of paper as Jake ran back up the steps and stormed into the room.

"Turn it back on! You won't belive this! It's George!" He said to Martha. Ray had turned the HAM radio back on. George was her younger brother and he was a HAM radio operator too.

"KE8ITZ, KE8ITZ, this is W8HB, can you hear me?" Jake smiled at the women, as he keyed the mike. Martha was stunned, her brother was alive? He lived with and was the primary caretaker for their mother, Helen. She was in her early 90's and had shown signs of Parkinson's and dementia.

"W8HB, this KE8ITZ and I read you loud and clear, but I don 't know how much juice we have left. How are you doing? Was Detroit hit?"

"That's great! We are doing ok, but yeah, the city is pretty much gone. Mom and I were sitting in the front room and I had just gotten up to use the bathroom. My back was turned when the bomb went off. I didn't see the flash, but I could feel the heat and see my shadow inside the house. The blast wave blew in the windows. We could see the mushroom cloud from the front yard. We have had some fires get close but they are out now. I boarded the windows up and at night there are people running around shooting guns. Not sure about much else. We are running on generator here and I have some supplies to get by for awhile." Jake's mind spun, if George and Helen were at home and felt the effects of the blast wave, then they were in danger from the fallout.

"That's good to hear. George, don't go outside for a while, give it seventy-two hours and even then don't touch anything that has a coating of dust. Do you copy that?" He waited for a response. Several moments later the speaker crackled to life.

"Copy that." George responded grimly. Jake decided to give him an update on their status.

"I am with Martha and Janey and their neighbor Ray, broadcasting from her house. We are all fine here and should be for the foreseeable future." Jake handed the mike to Martha and showed her how to work it.

"George, are you still there?"

"Martha? Yes, I'm here."

"How is mother?"

"Not good, I'm afraid. Like I said the shockwave from the blast was so violent that the front windows had blown in and she was cut pretty bad and her face was burnt. I did the best that I could, but I don't think she will last much longer. Along with the stress of everything else that is going on, it is taking it's toll."

"Please tell her I love her, and I love you to George. Thank you for being there with her." She handed the mike back to Jake.

"I know." George said quietly.

"Hey George, it's Jake again. We are going to sign off now, but I will be back on tomorrow morning at 8am. Talk to you then?"

"Sure, I'll be listening. W8HB, clear."

"KE8ITZ clear." Jake flipped the power switch and watched the radio display dim.

"Well that's that."

=================== * ===================

They worked in silence for the next few hours moving Martha's belongings and supplies to Ray's house. The work was made easier with many hands helping. Ray's son, Billy, stood guard at the door while they hustled and bustled about. Jake had met Billy before and knew that he was a Boy Scout. He mentioned to Ray that he is impressed with Billy's attitude and behavior during this time of upheaval.

"Thanks, Jake. I mean that. We have always tried to instill the proper morals and set the right example for our kids."

"You did a helluva job, Ray!" he smiled and smacked Ray on the back.

The last box of food was finally stored away and Jake tapped Janey on the shoulder. They had boxes everywhere, in the attic, in the basement, even in the garage. The boxes were stacked so that Ray's late 70's Volkswagen Van was almost hidden from view. It was a pet project of Ray's to get it running.

"Time to go." He turned to Ray and Kelly. "If you can get a vehicle working, nothing newer than the mid-80s, here is our address." He smiled and handed Ray a slip of paper with the address and set of directions. "If trouble comes your way and you need someplace to go, please don't hesitate." He smiled and shook their hands.

"Maybe now would be a good time to get that old van up and running. It seems that I have lots of time!" Ray smiled weakly. "Mr. Hawkins, do you think this is the end of times?" Billy had appeared at the doorway and had a look of deep worry and concern. Jake looked at their faces, all turned to him.

"No. It's not the end of times." He reassured them, "but it is a new beginning." Billy relaxed a little at that.

"Tell me son, are you an Eagle Scout yet?"

"No sir, not yet."

"What rank are you?"

"Life Scout, sir."

"So a Life Scout! Do you have an Eagle Project in mind?"

"Well, I was planning on making some benches around the park and maybe putting some trash containers in as well."

"Noble, very noble of you. Might I suggest a new project?" Jake asked.

"Sure, I guess." Billy was unsure about Jake, and what he might have in mind.

"Well, the times have changed since you first thought about your Eagle Project, right?"

"Yes sir."

"And your previous project was meant to beautify the park and provide places of rest for people, right?"

"Yes sir."

"I would think that now is the time for all of your scouting knowledge to be put to the test. Don't you think?"

"I am not sure I understand you, sir."

"Ok, did you earn the First Aid, Emergency Preparedness, and Wilderness Survival merit badges?"

"Yes sir, I did!"

"Good, I think in the next few months, you will be using all of the skills that you learned for those merit badges. If you would let me, I would like to challenge you." Billy looked to his parents, who only smiled and pointed back to Jake.

"I challenge you to change your Eagle Project from benches and trash cans, to keeping you and your family alive and well through the winter until next spring. Can you do it? Will you do it?" Billy was just as methodical as his father, and was slow to take action.

"I think I can, sir." He answered timidly.

"You think you can? Son, you need to know you can. Your family is depending on you. Depending on you to lead, to support and to guide them. So I ask again, can you do it?" Billy stood straighter and taller as he looked to his father and mother.

"Yes! I can and I will!" he answered confidently.

"Good Man!" Jake clapped him on the back and shook his hand in the scout way.

"I'll be back in the spring, God willing, and if you all are here and healthy I will proudly proclaim you Eagle Scout and present you with the award." They all smiled and gathered around Billy. Each giving him words of encouragement. Jake broke away and gently pulled Janey out of the fray.

"Janey, we should get going."

"Ok." Janey and Jake embraced Martha, each in turn taking a little longer than the last.

"I love you Mom!"

"I love you too, honey." Martha answered.

"I'll try to come by next week on bike and check on you. No matter what, listen to that radio!" They each said goodbye and headed out.

==================== * ====================

Billy lingered at the front windows watching the two people walk off. Ray, Kelly and Martha busied themselves with unpacking and beginning the long arduous task of inventorying the supplies.

"Dad, who was that man again?"

"That was Jake Hawkins, Martha's son-in-law, and the best Scoutmaster that I have ever seen!" Billy looked back at Jake and thinks, *Scoutmaster!?*

"He was a scoutmaster? Of what troop?"

"Troop 211, in town." In the few minutes that he interacted with him, Billy had compared Jake to his own scoutmaster of his troop. The two men couldn't be more polar opposite. Where his Scoutmaster was mousey and talked down to the scouts, Mr. Hawkins had charisma and seemed like a true leader. Billy looked back at the receding humanoid forms. *That is one Scoutmaster I could follow!*

CHAPTER 35

The journey was coming to an end and Jake could feel it. His feet were sore and his back ached. He was dirty and all he wanted was to take a nice hot shower, and sleep for a few days in his soft bed. *That will have to wait, need to get the kids first*, he thought.

He looked over at his wife, her soft auburn hair slightly obscuring her face as she struggled with her pack. It really wasn't her size, but in trying times, you make do. She brushed her hair back and saw him watching her, a smile swept across his face as blood rushed to hers. Even after eighteen years of marriage he could still make her blush with a smile.

"Shut up," she said while trying to hide her embarassment. He raised his hands to surrender. "I didn't say anything!"

"I know."

"Love you."

"Love you too." She really did love him, with all her heart and soul.

They walked in silence, listening to the birds and the occasional dog barking. His hiking stick clicked and

269

clacked on the asphalt. They had gone through Jiang-Li's bag and distributed the items that they could use between them. The hobo stick was gone and the hiking stick was back.

Among the trees and dormant subdivisions sat a collection of sprawling buildings. Once full of children and learning, now dark and seemingly vacant. Janey's heart started to race as her children's school finally came into view. Three of the local schools sat nestled close together, two elementaries and a middle school. They were separated by only a few hundred yards, an aquatic center and the old high school football field.

The middle school was their destination. The sprawling building was in a small valley. Behind it sat a rarely used baseball diamond and a soccer field. Across the parking lot, from the main entrance fo the middle school, sat the old football field. The same field that Jake and Janey used to march on back in the day with the high school marching band.

"Jake, look!" she pointed to the school and soon realized that he wasn't walking with her anymore. He had altered course and was beelining for one of the elementary schools. The elementary housed the lower grades, kindergarten through fifth grade. Ella had graduated last year and was now in the sixth grade at the middle school.

"Jake!? Where are you going? The kids aren't at that school anymore!" she called out to him.

"I know, but Beth could be. If she is, then she's coming with us." The realization that her neice, Elizabeth Hawkins, could be still be there struck Janey to her core. She covered her mouth in shock.

"Oh my God! Beth!" Her motherly instincts kicked in and she quickened her pace to catch up to Jake. Since they were so close she decided her kids could stand to wait a few minutes more.

A small playground bordered by a tall wrought iron fence, sat adjacent to the elementary school. The only way in to the playground was through the school interior to an exterior door. The exterior gates to the playground appeared to be securely chained and locked. *At least someone is thinking clearly,* Jake thought. Children of all sizes could be seen swinging and sliding, jumping and laughing. There were a few that were gathered on the benches, clearly homesick. Their noses and eyes red from crying.

Jake walked up to the fence and waved at one of the few adults that were monitoring the children. A young woman, with long dark hair and circles under her eyes approached him warily.

"Hello!" Jake called. The woman slowly approached the fence. She could see that Jake was armed and was cautious. He had the handgun tucked

271

into his waistband just above his belt buckle. She
stopped a few feet shy of the fence, well out of arms
reach.

"Hello. Can I help you?" she asked timidly.

"I hope so! I'm Jake Hawkins, this is my wife
Janey. Who is in charge here? I need to talk to someone
about finding my neice." She looked past Jake to Janey,
who smiled and waved.

"I'm Mrs. Johnson. You need to go the office, and
see Mrs. Young, the principal." The children had taken
notice of them and their curiosity got the better of them.
They ran for the fence, each wanting to see if it was their
parents that had come for them. They were sorely
disappointed when they saw that it wasn't. Janey wept
for them.

"Thank you. Sorry for the disruption." Jake
waved goodbye and took Janey gently by the arm. They
walked arm in arm up to the front office doors. Jake
took note that there were no barricades or chains here.
Not smart, he thought. He grabbed the door handle and
turned, hoping that it was locked, it wasn't. *Stupid.*
They stepped into the foyer and found the second
entrance door securely locked. *Better, but still not great.*
He peered through the small security window and could
see several men and women sitting around a desk. He
rapped several times on the door, drawing their
attention. A tall woman with short dark hair and small

silver glasses got up and approached the door. She smiled and let them in.

"Hello! What can I do for you? Are you here to pick up a student?"

"Yes, I am. Who are you?" Jake was pretty sure this was the principal. It wasn't that long ago his own children had attended this school. But verification could be useful.

"Well, I am Mrs. Young. Principal of this school. And you are?" She was confirmed. Jake introduced himself and Janey.

"We need Elizabeth Hawkins, a fifth grader. We don't know her teacher's name, I'm sorry."

"Are you her parents?" she asked now concerned.

"No. Aunt and Uncle. She is our neice, her father is my brother." Jake answered as he pulled out his wallet and took out his id. Janey followed suit and did the same. The principal looked them over and handed them to a small older woman who had approached the trio. The secretary looked them over and shuffled away to a desk.

"You will have to please bare with us. Since the computers are down it will take a few minutes to verify you and find Elizabeth's class. We may have to go room to room, but that would be very disruptive. You do understand?"

"Yes, I do. Thank you for your help," he said. She nodded and smiled, then motioned for them to sit down while they wait. They were more than happy to oblige. The old secretary returned and handed them their identification cards and a bottle of water. It wasn't cold, but it was wet, they took them and thanked her for the offering. Janey nudged Jake gently to get his attention. She tapped her nose and wrinkled it. He understood, took a deep breath through his nose and immediately wished he hadn't. The stench of sewage filled his sinuses. It was subtle, and wasn't overpowering. It was like smelling a barbeque on the breeze and not knowing where it was coming from. It was starting to get bad here.

"May I have a piece of paper and a pen?" Jake asked the secretary. She nodded and handed him a blue ballpoint and few sheets of printer paper.

Jake took the paper and was furiously scribbling on it. Janey was beginning to wonder if Beth had been picked up by her mother, Tracy, when a small child with dark brown hair and wide brown eyes walked into the room. She looked around the room, wondering why she was called out from class. Her gaze settled on the two tired forms sitting near the door.

"Uncle Jake! Aunt Janey!" She rushed over to them and they enveloped her into a long embrace. Janey showered her with kisses on her head and Jake touseled her hair.

"Well, I guess she knows you, so she can go."

"Thank you, Mrs. Young." Janey said.

"Janey, would you take Beth and get her belongings and anything useful from her locker." Janey nodded, took Beth by the hand, and exited the room out into the hallway.

"Mr. Hawkins? A word?"

"Yes Ma'am?" Jake answered as he shouldered his pack once more. She looked at him, unsure of how to start.

"Well, you see, it's like this. We don't really know what's going on out there, in the world. All we know is our own little world. Is there any advice you could give us?" Jake already had some thoughts on the matter.

"Ok, first, don't let anybody in the building, not even the vestibule. Too dangerous. Second, if someone comes for a student don't let that child anywhere near that adult until he or she can positively identify the adult. Sort of secondary verification on your part. Lastly, here." He handed her the piece of paper. On it he had written the date, his name, the name of the student, and his address.

"It's sort of an affidavit. All parties should sign it, including a school official. This may not be fool proof but it is a start."

"Thank you so much, Mr. Hawkins. It is far, far better than what we have been doing."

"You are most welcome, Mrs. Young. I fully understand the strain you are all under. I would hope that you are planning for the long haul."

"Why? What is going on out there? We have been visited by the police twice. They told us to stay in the school and wait for further instructions. That was two days ago." Jake took off his glasses and rubbed his eyes with the heels of his hands. He took a deep breath and told them what he knew.

================== * ==================

"Oh my God!" The principal said. The rest of the office staff were all in shock. They all stood in silence at the revelations Jake had given them.

"It's all true. Things are not what they once were. You should start rationing whatever food and water you have remaining. How many students do you have here? How are you holding up?" Mrs. Young only stood and stared, her mouth still agape. She was still in shock from his tale.

"Mrs. Young?" He snapped his fingers in front of her face to bring her back to the present. She blinked a few times and looked at him.

"I'm sorry, what did you say?" he repeated his questions to her, now fully aware.

"We have 204 students remaining. Many parents or guardians have already come and gotten their children. We don't really know what to do with the rest. They seem to be doing ok, many get homesick at night, when it gets dark. We do have about twenty or so students that have older siblings at the middle school and they desperately want to go over there. We have families of our own that we want to get home to as well." She waved her hand at the office staff, and the few teachers that had joined them in the now cramped office. "The teachers and myself are doing the best we can. The custodial staff has remained as well as a couple of the cafeteria staff."

"Good! Have the cafeteria staff inventory everything you have. The custodians need to get the water pumps going from the aquatics center and start flushing the toilets. I can smell them from here and I can only imagine what it is like in the bathrooms." She only nodded in embarassment.

"As for the middle school, we will be heading there next. I will talk with their staff and let them know that you are in need of help. I will suggest to the staff there, that they should combine with the other elementary school, pool the resources, as it were. This will alleviate the older sibling issue and maybe some of the homesickness. Stay strong, Mrs. Young. You and your staff are doing an outstanding job." They thanked Jake profusely and he responded in kind. With one last wave goodbye, he departed for the middle school.

CHAPTER 36

Janey and Beth had started for the middle school and were already a good distance ahead of Jake. He saw that they were holding hands and that did his weary heart some good. Adjusting his pack, he hurried to catch up.

The distance between the schools was only a couple of hundred yards, but after the last few days it felt like a mile. Jake's heart quickened at the thought of finally holding his children again. Suddenly the distance didn't seem as far.

The middle school was just a bit larger than the elementary school since it held the combined sixth through eight grade classes from two different elementary schools. Jake knew his way around this school as well, since he had attended it many years ago as a student. The teachers were different but the classes were laid out the same.

Jake caught up to the girls and was huffing and puffing quite terrible. The strain of the journey was taking its toll on him, and his asthma had begun acting up again. Janey saw the distress on his face and started to go to him. He waved her off as he pulled his inhaler from his pocket and shook it. He leaned on his hiking staff, thanking God that he had it with him to prop himself up. He breathed in the life giving medicine and held it. He expelled the air filling his lungs and looked at the small blue device in his hand and thought, *Jesus, I hope I have enough of these stored away!* He saw Janey and Beth staring at him, so he smiled back.

"I'm good now. Don't worry. C'mon! Let's go!" He strode past them and up to the front door of the school. Inside he could see the cafeteria, known as The Commons, was full of students and adults. He quickly scanned the group for his own children. Janey and Beth did the same, and it wasn't long before he spied a young blonde figure, with blue eyes standing taller than his classmates.

"I see Joey." He said.

"Where? I don't see him!" Janey sounded a touch frantic to Jake. He never broke his eye contact with his son, even as he spoke to his wife.

"Back right corner, standing with some kids I don't recognize, two girls and three other boys. Red shirt, torn blue jeans." Janey scanned the room for her son, finally the crowd parted enough she could see him.

"There he is!" She started waving and jumping up down, trying to get his attention. He had turned away, oblivious to the fact that his family was here.

The movement wasn't a total loss however, as another set of eyes recognized them. A young man, just bit over five feet tall, blonde and hazel eyes. Anthony Sommers, one of Jake's scouts, had lifted his head and saw the two adults standing before him in the vestibule.

"Mr. Hawkins?" he said out loud. Jake broke his gaze from Joey and shifted to Anthony, smiled and waved at him. Anthony stood up and walked to the glass doors.

"Anthony! Good to see you! Go get Joey!" Jake yelled through the glass, hoping to be understood. Anthony nodded, turned and began moving through the crowd to his classmate. As Jake watched him go, his heart began to race. Soon Anthony was at Joey's side, talking excitedly and pointing to the front of the Commons. Joey's eyes lit up when he saw his parents and cousin all standing there waving at him.

"DAD! MOM!" he yelled and pushed his way through the crowd. The other students were now aware that there were parents here. Each strained and stretched to see if it was their parents. The disappointed looks and slumped shoulders told Jake all he needed to know.

"DAD! MOM! Where have you been?" Tears streamed down his cheeks in joy at the sight of his parents. He desperately wanted them to hold him. He pushed on the door release, but it didn't move. Jake saw

281

that it was locked and chained. This angered him. *How could they lock these poor kids in here. The locks should be on the outer doors, not the ones inside!* He pointed to the main office, so Joey would know where he was going. The school office was situated off the main vestibule and the entryway sat wide open. One wall was shared with the Commons and was completely glassed in. Another door led into the Commons from the office, but it too was chained and locked.

"Excuse me? Who is in charge here? Where is Mr. Henriksen?" Jake's voice seemed to echo in the small room. He was desperately trying to keep his anger in check.

"Mr. Henriksen is in his office. May I ask who you are?" Said a small mousey woman, whose name plate read, Mrs. Bommarito.

"I am Jake Hawkins, parent of two students that attend school here." She slowly rose up, trying to decide if he was a threat to her or the children. The handgun protruded from his waistband. She could see from the expression on his face that he meant business, but if it was ill or not, she did not know.

"I'll go get him." She turned and hurried away.

"Thank you," he growled through clenched teeth.

"Are you here for a student?" Asked another mousey woman, this one was much older. Jake recognized but couldn't remember her name at the moment.

"Yes, two actually. Ella and Joey Hawkins. She's in the sixth grade and he is in the eighth."

"Do you have any identification?" Again, he produced his driver's license, and handed it over to the staff member. After checking it, she decided that he was who he said he was and handed it back. She then slid a clipboard with a handwritten form to him. He read it over and saw that it asked for much of the same information that he had instructed the previous school staff to gather. He filled it out and slid it back to her. She took it, read it over, satisfied that it was complete she slid it into a manila folder.

"I just came from the elementary school and they are in need of assistance." Jake explained what was happening there and suggested that they should get together with the other elementary to combine resources and decide on a proper way to track who had picked up a child from their care. The secretary jotted down all of Jake's suggestion but was shaking her head.

"I think your ideas are wonderful, Mr. Hawkins, however, Mr. Henriksen is in charge here and he makes the decisions." Jake's temper was beginning to flare.

"Okay, so, where is Mr. Henriksen?" Jake demanded.

"I'm here!" Mr. Henriksen was a short, heavy set man, with thinning hair and slumped shoulders, he could have been a lawyer or an accountant in a different life. Jake stepped forward and offered his hand. Mr. Henriksen sized him up, and shook his hand with a monstrous ferocity. He was trying to intimidate Jake, with his grip and force. Jake knew that he would be able to take this man in a fair fight. A stiff wind would be able to blow him over.

"Hello, Mr. Henriksen." Jake introduced him self and his wife.

"I am here for my kids." The principal turned to his staff, who in turn murmured that the proper forms had been filled out and filed. He motioned to another man, that had appeared from the hallway. This one was much taller and thinner than Henriksen.

"Mr. Smith, please bring....?" He looked to Jake for the names.

"Ella and Joey Hawkins," Jake replied.

"Yes, please bring Ella and Joey Hawkins to the office at once. Try to be discreet."

"Yes sir." He responded.

"Hold on!" Jake interjected. "My son is right there!" He pointed out into the common area at his son, who was standing against the glass. Jake noticed that he wasn't alone. Several of his scout mates are with him.

"Mr. Smith, bring him in here, but no one else!" Henriksen commanded. Smith nodded, shuffled to the locked door, produced a set of keys, and proceeded to unlock the door. Joey stood on the other side, anxious to get to his parents. As soon as the door opened, Joey flew into the waiting arms of Jake and Janey. They showered him with love and kisses.

"Where is Ella?" Janey asked Joey.

"I don't know. I haven't seen her in a couple days! We have been kept separate from the other grades and the teachers won't let us see each other. None of us who have brothers or sisters are allowed to be together!" Joey informed his father, as he struggled to keep his emotions in check. Jake's anger and rage were at a boiling point. He turned on the staff. Mr. Smith stood stupidly by the door, as he started to relock the chains.

"Is this true?" His eyes flared with hate and aggression. Mr. Henriksen saw this and was momentarily taken back.

"Y-y-y-yes. It's true, but it was for the safety of the students," he stammered.

"Joey, I want you to go and get Ella, Anthony Sommers, Andy Black, and both of the Mitchell kids. Bring them back with their backpacks and jackets. Go. Now."

"Ok, dad." Joey tried to push past Smith but Henriksen was faster.

"Hold on! NO! You are only to sign out your children! Who are these others you are talking about?"

"They are my scouts, and my responsibility now. It appears that you are running a prison and I will NOT have my kids stay here another minute!" Jake was slowly advancing on the shrinking principal. Joey saw this and was in awe of his father.

"MY SON WILL GET MY DAUGHTER AND NO ONE WILL STOP HIM! DO YOU UNDERSTAND ME, MR. HENRIKSEN?" Jake bellowed, his rage finally taking over him. Mr. Smith had dropped the lock and retreated from the doorway.

"Joey! GO!" said Janey. Joey nodded and pushed through the door to the common area. He quickly grabbed Anthony who had been watching the encounter. Joey explained the mission while Anthony listened. Once all was relayed, they each took off in opposite directions. Before long, a group of young men and a small girl with bleach blonde hair and hazel eyes were streaming through the door to the office.

"Dad, I got Ella and the guys." Joey said as they came through.

"Hi daddy!" Ella said as she was swept up into Janey's protective embrace. Jake hadn't taken his eyes off of Henriksen.

"Hello princess!" He said warmly. "Anthony, Andy have you seen your brothers in the last couple of days?"

Anthony and Andy each had a younger sibling attending the school, Brendan Sommers and Garret Black were sixth graders while the older boys were in the eighth grade.

"No, Mr. Hawkins." They responded together. Jake glared even more at the cowering principal. His nostrils flared and his breathing was loud enough for all to hear.

"Go and get your brothers and their gear. Hurry."

"Yes sir." They smiled and took off like bullets from a rifle.

"Joey, did you find the Mitchell kids?" he asked. Before his son could respond, one of the secretaries piped up. She pulled out a wrinkled piece of paper and read from it.

"Dexter and Randy Mitchell? Their mother picked them two days ago."

"Thank you, Mrs. Bommarito." Jake said, his gaze was still locked on the cowering principal. "Joey, I want you and two other fellows grab a bottle of water from the cafeteria for everyone. Understand? One bottle per person. Go!" Joey nodded and tapped two of his friends and they were through the door like the wind.

Mr. Henriksen was seething, not only was this man, this stranger, taking his children, but now he was taking his supplies.

"YOU CANNOT DO THIS! YOU ARE ONLY SUPPOSED TO TAKE YOUR OWN CHILDREN! NOT MY WATER OR ANY OTHER STUDENTS!" Henriksen had found some courage. Jake sneered back at the man, clearly not scared. He spoke carefully and deliberately.

"I CAN do this and I am. Mr. Henriksen, you can be in charge of whatever this is. I can tell you that I am a Scoutmaster of a local boy scout troop. These young men are my scouts. I have spent countless days and nights protecting them and watching over them. On those excursions I am their guardian. I am their parent. I am no longer asking permission. I will be taking these children into my care, and there isn't a DAMN THING YOU CAN DO ABOUT IT!"

Mr. Henriksen finally defeated, stepped back and plopped down in a nearby chair. The only sound heard was the sound of the children in the Commons, now alerted to the fracas taking place in the office.

"Mr. Hawkins, what should we do now?" Mrs. Bommarito asked. She had recognized that he might be their only hope to survive this. Jake took a deep breath and looked at the office staff, really looked at them. Their faces were streaked and dirty, their hair was all disheveled and in disarray. Their clothing was stained in the armpits and wrinkled. He truly felt that they were trying their best, but their leader was misguided.

"May I have a few pieces of paper?" He asked quietly. She nodded and slid a few sheets across the desk to him. He quickly jotted the same instructions that he already given the elementary school staff.

"I would also start looking up the address of the older students. If they live close by and have a house key, they should be allowed to go. Also, any siblings should be allowed to be together." He ended with his name, address, and the list of all the scouts that he was taking with him. He noticed that the doorway to Commons stood ajar and the students were jockeying for a better position to hear.

"I am taking guardianship of any scouts that wish to come with me. If they do not, they are free to stay here." He said louder for all to hear. Behind him he heard a few young voices whispering their agreement. He turned and saw his scouts and his family all grinning widely. *They are all happy to see me.* Two of the youngest started towards him, but Jake held them back.

"Wait a minute. I want you all to identify me" They young men all look at each other and in one voice yell out.

"MR. JAKE HAWKINS!"

"How do you know me?" He asked, clearly proud of his young charges. Again they answered together,

"SCOUTS!"

================== * ==================

The remaining students in the Commons heard the yelling and were pleading with Jake and Janey to take them too. They were causing quite the ruckus. Mr. Henriksen glared at Jake, willing him to understand that this was what he was trying to avoid. Jake quickly stepped into the doorway before the children could rush in.

"QUIET DOWN! QUIET!" he yelled. "LISTEN TO ME! YOU HAVE TO SETTLE DOWN!" The young crowd slowly calmed enough that Jake didn't have to yell. All eyes were upon Jake as he spoke.

"Listen, all of you. You are all a vital part of a scared new world. The power is out and may never come back on. Yes, you will be sad that you can no longer play video games or watch movies, but that should not stop you from having fun and learning. These few young men and women that are leaving, are leaving for a life full of work and worry. You are far safer here than out there."

"But we miss our mom's and dad's!" a small voice cried out.

"I know you are, I know you are, and I am sure that they miss you, too. They would want you to be safe, and that is what you are here. I spoke with the teachers at one of the elementary schools and if anyone has a little brother or sister there, then the staff members of both schools will work to get reunited!" He watched some faces light up at that.

"It will take some time for this process to work. Please be patient. Eighth graders! It is up to you to help the teachers and staff. Do not be a part of the problem, be a part of the solution!" Jake looked out at the now calmed crowd and felt that more than a few of them have grown up a little today. *This is the youth of a new America. Oh boy,* he thought.

Jaked walked back into the office and asked the secretaries for forms for each of the students he was taking. After signing and dating each one, he grabbed his pack, hiking stick and started to leave. Janey had taken the rag tag group of kids out of the office and into the courtyard in the front of the school. Mr. Henriksen grabbed his arm gently and held him back a moment. His eyes darted back and forth nervously.

"What else can we do? We are running out of water and food!" Jake looked at the now defeated man, and sympathy welled up inside him.

"Get with your science teachers and custodians. Come up with some ways to gather water from the rain. Purify it, filter it, even boil it for three minutes if you have to. You might even want to send out gathering parties to the closest houses that are now vacant. I would grab pillows, and bedding, first aid kits, toiletries and shoes. Set it all up in the gym and start a trading post with anyone that comes by. This is a brave new world, Mr. Henriksen. Be brave too." Jake held out his hand and the principal took it in his. A true understanding between them and mutual respect was left unspoken, but felt.

"One last thing, Mr. Henriksen, I hope you understand that the times are changing and that you should work closely with the other schools here. Any police officer that comes to visit should be treated with caution if you don't recognize them. ANYONE can put on a uniform. Ask for identification before allowing entry. Do not allow the student to go with anyone they do not know. The safety of our children is our only hope for a bright future." The principal nodded and wiped the tears from his eyes.

"Thank you Mr. Hawkins. Good Luck." Jake nodded and turned to Janey and his troop. They stood hand in hand, a real solid family unit. It was clear to him that she wouldn't be letting go any time soon. His family and scouts all smiled and rushed to Jake as soon as he was clear of the school. Janey raised her eyebrows at the group of teens and preteens, wondering how they were going to survive now!

CHAPTER 37

"Thank you Mr. Hawkins!" The scouts all spoke at once as they hugged Jake tightly. Suddenly they all spoke as one. The questions flew fast and furious at him. He put up his hands to quiet them.

"Guys, hey guys, quiet down!" Jake pleaded. They continued to pepper him with questions about their parents and families. They too wanted to know about the ongoing catastrophe. He tried again to quiet them, but they weren't listening.

"SCOUTS!" Joey suddenly yelled. He was standing next to Janey, his hand raised in the three fingered Scout Salute. They all turned to the sound and each raised their hands in salute, quieting down instantly.

"Thank you, Joey." Jake looked proudly at his son.

"You're welcome, dad." He smiled sheepishly.

"Ok, here is the drill. Since Andy and Garret live closest, we will be going there first." A few of the scouts started to grumble with discontent.

"HEY! There will be none of that! This isn't like one of our weekend excursions. This is real and it is scary. Now, once we get them safely home, then we will work on getting you all home or at least in touch with your parents. So for the time being, I am your new guardian. Joey would you be our Senior Patrol Leader?" He asked his son, hoping that Joey would accept. Joey looked up at his mom for some motherly advice or maybe an excuse to get out of it. Janey smiled proudly. He looked back at his dad and took in a deep breath.

"Yeah, I'll be SPL." The rest of the group smiled and applauded him. They were relieved that Mr. Hawkins hadn't asked them. Jake beamed proudly and handed him the hiking staff.

"Great! This is the staff of leadership. Whoever holds it, is the leader and you will listen to his or her orders. Got it?"

"YES SIR!" They all shouted in unison.

"Andy? Lead us to your house. You and Joey take point and everyone else fall in behind, make two lines and keep your heads up."

"Yes sir!" Andy and Joey worked together to form them up and get them moving out. Janey, and the girls were hanging out near the rear of the pack, waiting for Jake. She approached him as their group started walking.

"What are you thinking?!" she asked him innocently. He looked at her, shocked.

"What?"

"You complained about bringing Jiang-Li, but it's okay to bring these kids with us? She was one mouth to feed, now we have six or seven? I just don't understand you." She threw up her hands in disgust.

"I was upset about bringing her along, but I couldn't leave her there with Francis and I figured that she might be able to us out along the way. Why are you mad?"

"I'm not mad! I just want to know what your plan is. I know you have a plan, because you wouldn't have brought all these kids along with us without a plan!"

"Honey, I just couldn't stand by and watch these promising young men stay in that school! I know where most of them live and I can probably help them get home. If not, then we can raid the nearby houses for things we might need. I do have an inkling of a plan. It isn't great, but it is something. I just need to take stock first." She grasped his hand tightly and gently kissed him. His was a heart of gold.

"Ok, good thinking, keep it up, Mr. Scoutmaster." She said coyly.

=================== * ===================

The remaining trip to the Black house went quickly, since the kids were jabbering away loudly. *Well, at least they are outside and away from the school,* Jake thought. He doubted if any of them would ever return to that school.

"MR. HAWKINS!" someone yelled from the front of the group. The group had stopped and and were all facing a large two story cape cod style house. A few of them were pointing at one of the upstairs windows. Jake looked up at it and immediately yelled for them stop looking and to get moving.

"What is it? What's going on?" Janey asked.

"Cover Ella's and Beth's eyes, they don't need to see this." Jake said in hushed tones.

"What? What is it?"

"A body. Someone hung themselves and you can see it through the window. To make it worse, there is blood on the window. Possibly from a gunshot. A second body? I don't know."

"Oh no! That's horrible."

"Yeah. It is. Come on, keep moving." They walked on in silence, the only sound was their footsteps and the clicking of the hiking stick on the concrete sidewalk echoing off the houses. The occasional dog bark could be heard inside some of the homes. Each one tugged at Jake's heart and he couldn't help but worry about his own canine companions waiting for him at home.

"There it is! My house!" Andy said as he started running. The rest of the group followed, much to Jake's consternation.

"WAIT! SCOUTS! WAIT!" His pleas fell on deaf ears as they all ran for their friends house. Jake could see Andys' moms' jeep sitting in the driveway. *Maybe she made it home before it happened,* he thought. Andy and Garret had made it to the front door before everyone else and were banging away.

"MOM! IT'S US! OPEN UP!" Andy and Garret yelled. Their youthful impatience won out and they ran to the back of the house, hoping to get in through the doorwall. Before Jake could stop them, he saw the front door open and a visibly shaken Stephanie Black step out. Jake knew Stephanie from the troop. She was on the committee and helped out at every fundraiser and service project. They had a close, friendly relationship and had poked fun at each other on many occasions. He could tell that this was not the time for fun. Her blue eyes were red and bloodshot, it was clear that she had been crying hard. Her blonde hair hung in oily strands around her face and her skin glistened with sweat.

"MOM!! WE'RE HERE!" Andy and Garret had seen Stephanie through the glass door wall. Stephanie ran to the back door and slid it open. She wrapped her children in the biggest bear hug that Jake had ever seen. The rest of the troop stood by and watched the scene unfold, each thinking of their own parents and loved ones. Some wiped away tears or maybe a mote of dust that had found its way into their eyes.

"Oh my God! Andy! Garret! How did you get out? I thought the school was in lock down and no one would be able to get you out!" She held her boys and wiped away their tears with her hands. She brushed their hair with her fingers and checked them out for any bumps, bruises or injuries.

"It was Mr. Hawkins that got us out, Mom! You should have seen it!" Andy said.

"Yeah! He was awesome! He yelled at Mr. Henriksen, cuz he wasn't going to let us go, but then Mr. Hawkins growled at him and he scared Mr. Henriksen real bad!" Garret was clearly in awe of Jake. They went on to describe the conditions in the school and what they went through in the last few days. Stephanie listened intently, both shocked and appalled.

"I just can't believe that the teachers and principal at the school would treat the students that way!" Jake explained that they were just as scared as everyone else and the local government wasn't giving any guidance.

"The only thing that matters now, is that my boys are home. Thank you so much!" She said as she embraced Jake, fresh tears began to flow but this time it was from the adults. He held her as she wept, and glanced at Janey. She looked back at him, with raised eyebrow and crossed arms. Jake suddenly felt very uncomfortable, so he cleared his throat and stepped back from Stephanie. She sniffled and wiped her eyes with the heels of her hands.

"I don't know what I would do without you! You are just too kind. Thank you so much!" Jake wasn't used to this many compliments, so he shrugged and shuffled his feet. Janey laughed at his embarassment and awkwardness. He shot Janey a hard look that said enough. She stuck her tongue out at him in defiance, and then winked.

"Stephanie, what is your situation here? Do you have anything prepared?" Jake said as he looked around her kitchen.

"Well, not much really. We have some canned food, mostly fruit cocktail, and some soup. I know we have some dried beans and pasta. Maybe some potatoes, I don't really know."

"What about water? Do you have any stored away? What about bottles of water?"

"Yeah, we have two cases in the garage, Larry prefers to take a couple when he runs." The sudden thought of her husband caused her throat to hitch. Jake caught on quickly. He looked to Janey who understood as well. She stepped closer to Stephanie and put her arm around her. Jake called out.

"Andy! Garret!" The kids had all run off to their rooms to show their friends their toys and personal items. Andy and Garret bounded into the room.

"Yes, Mr. Hawkins?"

"Ok, guys, your first mission. I want you to scour the house and garage for anything that will hold water. Empty milk jugs from the recycling, pop bottles, or even buckets. Ask some of the other guys to help."

"On it!" They said in unison and took off. Jake smiled and turned back to Stephanie.

"Stephanie, have you heard from Larry?" He asked softly. She tried to hold back some internal grief, but it poured forth in great gasping sobs. She shook her head from side to side to answer him. Janey held her a bit tighter and looked to Jake for reassurance. He had none.

"Stephanie, I'm sure that Larry is ok. He would be making every effort to get back to you and the boys." She only shook her head harder.

"NO! He's probably already dead! I was talking to him on the phone when it happened. He was driving on the freeway, going back to work after lunch. The last thing he said was something about a great big flash and then he was gone!" Jake feared that he may have been caught in the blast zone.

"Stephanie, where does Larry work?" Janey probed.

"He works for an architecture firm. They are based in Detroit, near the Renaissance Center." Janey looked to Jake, he only shook his head.

"I was at work too, and my mind won't shut off! I can't help thinking of what could have happened to him. Did he have an accident and is he hurt in the car? Is he dead? I don't know!" Jake sighed heavily and took her hands in his. He told her what he already knew about the nuclear explosion.

"Larry was probably caught in the blast. It would have been quick and painless." This caused her to wail and collapse. Jake and Janey held her as all three sat down hard on the floor. Together they mourned. They mourned for each other, and the world. They mourned for their children and their old lives now lost. Jake thought of Larry's contributions at scouting events. He attended every summer camp and would go running every morning. He helped out whenever Jake needed him to.

"Mr. Hawkins?" Andy was back with the scouts. "We have as many bottles and jugs and buckets as we could find. What do want us to do with them?" Jake untangled himself from the group and stood up and wiped his eyes. He coughed once to clear his throat.

"Put them in the garage for now. Next we need as many candles as we can find, and any working flashlights."

"Ok! On it!" Andy ran to Joey and told him what was next. Joey quickly divided up the tasks and they were off. Janey and Stephanie had regained their footing as well and had sat down at a large oaken table in the dining area off the kitchen. Jake found a scrap of paper and began to scribble on it. When he was done he went to them. Sitting across from the women, he slid the paper to Stephanie.

"If you need anything, anything at all, you can count us." She looked down at the paper and immediately recognized his address. Below it was another address and a series of instructions on how to find it.

"I know your address, but where is this other place?" she asked.

"It's my mother's property. It isn't much, but we may have to relocate. If we do, that's where we'll be."

"Thank you. Oh my gosh! Thank you!" She started to cry again.

"Stephanie, I need you to hold it together now. For Andy and Garret. They need you, and you need them."

"You're right. I'm sorry." She took a deep breath and steadied herself. He looked her in the eyes.

"No." The answer took her by surprise.

"No?" she asked.

"Don't be sorry. Be strong." he said with firm commitment.

"Be strong. Okay. I can do that." She said to herself.

"Good. Now then. How long have you been home?"

"I don't know, probably about a half hour before you all showed up. I started out walking but then I had to steal a bicycle and I rode home. I was going to go get the boys after I cleaned up and rested for an hour or so." She felt ashamed after saying it.

"What about the jeep? Does it run?" Jake asked.

"I don't know. I carpooled with a friend the day it started. I haven't even tried it. Do you think it will work?"

"I don't know. Where are the keys?" She was already digging through her purse before the question left his lips. The sparkle of life had returned to her eyes as she lifted them free and tossed them to Jake. Andy had found the adults and reported his mission success.

"Mr. Hawkins, we have the candles and the empty containers are in the garage."

"Great news! Now, one last thing. I need a garden hose. It has to be somewhat new, not old and cracked. Look for a dark green hose. If you don't have

one on your house, check the neighbors, but be careful!"
The scout nodded and ran off. Jake, Janey and Stephanie
walked outside to the jeep. Jake slid into the driver's
seat, expecting the worst, but hoping for the best. Before
he put the key in the ignition he looked up. The dome
light was on, but was very dim. *Not a bad sign, really*, he
thought. The engine cranked over once, twice, then
clicked. Each time it clicked the dome light flickered.

"Bad battery or blown fuse. But promising!" He
said to Stephanie.

"What do you mean promising?" He explained
the basics of an EMP and what the nuclear blasts did to
all electronics.

"So if this jeep had a replacement battery it might
run! That's the good news. The bad news is the fuel. I
am not sure how much you have in the tank, but it might
be worth it to try and scavenge any you can find."

"How would we do that?" she asked.

"Mr. Hawkins! We have everything in the
garage! Come and see!" Andy was back and this time
he had Joey with him. Jake smiled and Stephanie as he
locked the door to the jeep. He saw Janey glance at her
watch and back to Jake. *I know, I know! The dogs still need
us and our own kids are getting restless.*

"Ok, time for water harvesting. Everyone follow
me!" Jake called out. Once inside the dimly lit garage

Jake picked up one of the candles, pulled out his Zippo lighter and lit it. He handed it off to Joey.

"Here, light a few more candles, but not all of them!"

"Got it dad!" Joey already had an unlit candle in his hand.

"Andy, hand me that hose." He pointed to the long coiled length of dark green garden hose. Andy picked it up and handed it to Jake. He slid it through his hands until he found the end he was looking for, then he stretched the hose across his body from finger tip to finger tip. It was a basic measure for length. Satisfied that he had about six feet, he pulled out his folding knife and cut the hose. He tossed the remaining coil off to the side, and kept the smaller length.

"Okay, now everyone grab a container and if Mrs. Black would be so kind as to show us the way to the hot water tank!" He motioned for Stephanie to lead the way by handing her a candle. She graciously accepted it and led them all into the house and down into the basement. He noticed his wife was hanging back again.

"What was that all about?" Janey was getting antsy, *and a possibly a bit jealous*, he thought.

"What was what all about?" he asked as he stuck his tongue out at her, and winked.

Together they walked down into the darkened basement like a celtic funeral procession, every other person holding a candle before them. Soon they were all gathered around the hot water heater. The tall grey cylinder stood next to the now inert furnace. Both appeared to run on gas, which was good, if there was still pressure in the lines.

Jake gently made his way to the center of the group and began to describe the basic parts of the heater.

"Down near the bottom of the tank is the clean out valve. What does it look like to you?" He asked the group.

"An outdoor faucet? Like the one on the side of our house!" Garret was the first to respond.

"Exactly! Great job Garret! It is called a spigot. They both work the same. Turn the handle and water comes out. Now, since this is down low on the tank, there might be some sediment or muck or gunk, so we will drain that off into this low point drain." He had connected his length of hose to the spigot and had taken the other end to a hole in the floor covered by a dull white plastic grate. He turned the handle slowly and pointed to the drain. As everyone watched a slow trickle of brown colored water began to pour forth from the hose. Soon it lightened and was coming out clear, and he closed the valve.

"Okay, now stick that end into a container!" Jake was getting excited. He always got that way when he was teaching his scouts a new skill or concept. Joey picked up the cut hose end and stuck it into a milk jug. Jake turned the handle fully and water gushed out into the container. It filled rapidly and just before it overflowed, Jake closed the valve again. Joey carefully pulled the hose out and capped the jug. The rest of the group was in awe. They just witnessed their Scoutmaster harvest clean drinking water from a hot water tank. Jake grinned widely as he took in their astonishment.

"Jeez, guys this is Emergency Preparedness 101!! Most houses have a hot water heater that holds between thirty-five and forty gallons of clean drinking water." Jake stepped back and let them continue filling the rest of the containers.

Stephanie began to cry again, but this time it was tears of joy.

"Okay, now I wouldn't think of the kids knowing that, but I'm a grown ass adult and I didn't know about this! Thank you again! You are awesome, Jake! I am so glad we know you!" She wrapped her arms around Jake and planted a big kiss on his cheek. He saw that Janey was not happy with this turn of events. He quickly separated himself from Stephanie.

"Ok, no worries! Thank you! We have to go, but before we do, let's go back upstairs." They made their way out of the darkened basement and emerged into the muted light of a cloudy day.

"Get ALL of your canned and dry goods together. Inventory it all, start cooking any meat you have in your freezer or fridge. The refrigerator is no longer a cooling device, but a breeding ground for mold and fungus. Eat what you can , and start a composting pile in the corner of the yard, furthest from the house. It can be used for planting in the spring months. Got it all?" She had been furiously writing down all of Jake's instructions as he spoke. She nodded that she did.

"Mr. Hawkins!" Garret had appeared at his side. Jake looked down and smiled at the young man.

"Yes, Garret?" he asked.

"The containers are full, should we bring them back up to the garage, or..." he trailed off, not knowing what to do or say after that.

"No, son. Leave them down in the basement where it is cool. Tell Andy to close off the valve and take off the hose. Save the rest for another day and use it only as needed! Got it?" He asked the young boy. Garrett nodded and ran back down the stairs yelling for Andy. He turned back to Stephanie who had just finished writing.

"All good?" She looked up at him and smiled for the first time since they had arrived.

"Yes. I think we are all good. Now." Jake smiled back at her, happy to see that she would be fine, in time.

"JOEY!" he yelled for his son. The tall blonde haired boy appeared a the top of the basement steps.

"Yeah dad?"

"Get everyone together, we are heading out."

"On it." He disappeared back into the darkness. Jake could hear his son giving out orders to his peers. He couldn't be more proud of him.

Once everyone had gathered outside the modest home, Jake and Janey turned to Stephanie.

"Stephanie, I don't know if you have any firearms in the house and I don't need to know, but if you do, I would train Andy on how to use them."

He looked at the two young boys who were on the fast path to manhood.

"Guys, it is up to you to take care of your mother. You are the men of the house now. Andy, I know you used to play combat style video games. I want you to start thinking about security and safety for your family. If you need help, you know where I live." He shook the young man's hand.

"Well, we are outta here. Take care of yourselves." Jake stepped off the porch and waved at them.

"Goodbye Stephanie and good luck!" Janey added.

The young boys and girls in the group all waved goodbye to Andy, Garret and Mrs. Black, hoping that they would meet again some day. *Next stop, the Sommer's.*

CHAPTER 38

A half hour later the troop arrived at the Sommer's household. A tall two story structure, clad in alternating brown and tan brick with matching trim. Jake had three of the Sommers boys in his troop, Anthony, Brendan, and Steven. Steven was in the tenth grade and attended the high school.

"Ok, Anthony, and Brendan up front and with me, the rest of you stay here. Joey, get them quiet." Jake instructed as he took off his pack and kissed Janey on the cheek.

"Ok, dad!" Joey said as Anthony and Brendan said their goodbyes to the group. A few of the boys shook hands, the rest gave out hugs. Once they were done, Jake and the boys walked up to the front door.

"Do you have a key, by chance?" he asked Anthony.

"No, I don't. Steven is usually home before us. Jake nodded, turned and knocked twice. A small white dog appeared at the side window and started barking. Jake turned back to his group and shrugged, Janey

motioned to knock again. Jake rolled his eyes and
turned back to the door.

"I saw that!" Janey called out from the sidewalk.

"Of course you did." Jake mumbled as he
rapped again, but this time much harder. Inside they
could hear a rhythmic thumping and soon the door
locked clicked and swung open.

"Anthony! Brendan! You guys are home!"
Steven rushed out and embraced his brothers. It would
have been funny if it was any other day. The oldest of
the Sommers boys rarely showed even the slightest
inclination that he cared for his younger siblings, but in
even the darkest of times, family was what mattered
most.

Steven was the oldest of the three, he was the
same height as his younger siblings. All three had the
same blonde hair and blue eyes, save for Brendan who
wore glasses. During troop meetings, they stayed away
from each other, and it was a chore to get them to work
together.

"Hi, Mr. Hawkins! Thanks for bringing my
brothers home!" Steven blurted out. "Have you been to
Lincoln Elementary? My little sister Savannah is there."
He had seen Beth and Ella standing by Janey.

"No I haven't. I have been to the other
elementary school, and they are working to get their
children to homes. If you go there, mention my name

and that should give you some leverage. Oh and go together! Lash a wagon to a bike or something to make your journey quicker!" Jake leaned in close and whispered, "You might want to bring some protection as well. I know you like knives, and that should do for now. No guns! At least not yet. Got it?" Steven nodded.

"Ok, thanks!"

"Steven, are you guys ok here? Supplies wise?"

"Oh, yeah. As soon as I got home I took stock of our stuff and moved it all down to the basement. Cool and dark, ya know? We even have water stored in big jugs down there."

"Sounds like you are good to go then. Listen, if you need anything at all, you know where I live right?" The Sommers all had been to Jake's house before for troop projects and meetings.

"Yeah, I do! Thanks, Mr. Hawkins. Really, I mean it." He stuck out his hand. Jake took it and shook it firmly, not as a scout to man, but man to man. As Jake turned to leave, he could hear Anthony and Brendan already going through the process they performed at Andy's house.

================== * ==================

HOME BOUND

Almost home! Jake thought and unconsciously picked up his pace as his destination loomed before him. He watched his group of young charges cross the last major road before his own neighborhood. He once more counted them off, as he had done so many times before Tim and Eric Roberts, Adam Murphy Jr., Luke Johnson, Joey, Ella, Beth, and Janey. It was good to see the boys all taking and behaving like they should. The girls all walked together holding hands and looking both ways before crossing the street, some things that they used to do, now seem slightly trivial.

Jake spied a line of teenagers walking slowly along the highway, coming from the sprawling high school that was half a mile down the road to the north. The high school had been built ten years prior and housed almost a thousand students. Jake hoped that the school had a plan and weren't just letting the kids leave. That could be disastrous.

"Mr. Hawkins? LUKE?!?!" A tall, but stocky, young man with dark hair and glasses called out to the group. Luke spun about at the sound of his name and scanned the crowd until he spied a familiar face.

"JEFFREY??" He called out. Jeffrey Johnson was Luke's older brother and also in Jake's troop. The two brothers ran to each other. Luke jumped into his brothers outstretched arms. Jake smiled, so much hugging and reuniting today, it made him feel good and

315

have hope for humanity. He motioned to his group to hold and wait for him. This was met with much grumbling and belly aching.

"Jeffrey! Good to see you! How are you doing? What's going on at the high school?"

"Mr. Hawkins, good to see you too! Why is Luke with you? I'm doing good. The teachers and staff are just letting the kids go whenever they want to. I stayed for the last few days because I left my keys at home and I was hoping my mom would have come to get me and Luke. But I see that she hasn't." Jake informed him of the conditions at the lower schools.

"I took in Luke when I saw what was going on, but now you are here!" Jake hoped Jeffrey picked up what he was laying down.

"Hey, Mr. Hawkins! Jeffrey! I have a house key! Mom gave me one last year, in case I ever had to walk home!"

"LUKE! Oh my god! Come on, Let's go home! Is that okay, Mr. Hawkins?"

"Sure Jeffrey, but if you need any help or someplace to go, my door is open." Again, these young men had been to his house enough, no directions were needed. They waved goodbye and took off for home.

Home. Jake's home was only a few hundred yards away. It had been almost three days of constant walking, some sleeping, some fighting, and most of all:

surviving. *Three days of survival, I just might sleep that long when we get home,* Jake thought. The group cut through a yard or two and soon the small one story ranch bungalow was in sight. It was just big enough for the four of the Hawkins, but now they were eight. It would be tight, to be sure, but they would survive.

The group had begun jogging, some full tilt running to the house, and Jake found himself trying to jog too, but his legs and lungs just would not cooperate. Walking over fifty miles would do that to a person. The bundle of kids swarmed the porch and only parted for Janey as she dug through her pack and purse for the keys to the door. She scratched her head and looked up at Jake, who had just made it to the front yard and was huffing and puffing again. She waved at him to come up there, and instructed the group to back up.

"OK, EVERYONE take a few steps back. I know we are all anxious to get inside, but we have two dogs that have been home for the past three days. Alone. It could be quite messy in there. Let's send in Mr. Hawkins first to assess the mess, OK?" Her suggestion was met with a round of approval and look of disgust from the girls. Janey laughed when she saw Jake's face. Complete and utter defeat, but also a resignation and determination. Jake wanted to be the first to enter anyway. He dug out his keys and slid it into the lock. The deep barking of Samantha could be heard inside.

He immediately noted the absence of Billie's bark. Taking a deep breath, he turned the handle and stepped in.

The assault on his nostrils was intense. Only less intense was the canine attack on his legs and torso. Samantha rushed to greet Jake as he walked in. He knelt down and hugged her, scratching her back and face. She licked his face and hands, and rubbed her self on his legs. He turned and opened the door so she could get outside and meet the group. Janey shot him a look of concern, *Billie?* Her look said. He shook his head from side to side, once, *no Billie.*

Billie was their older dog, fifteen years old, which was positively ancient for a golden retriever. She was far past the average life expectancy for that breed. He closed the door gently and began a search for his beloved dog.

The stench of feces and urine wafted around him like a dense rolling fog. There was something else, under all the unpleasantness that he couldn't yet identify. *Moldy food?* He thought. *No, that's not it.*

Moving from room to room, he spied several dog piles and lot of garbage strewn across the carpet. *Great, they got into the trash!* He knew they would, but it was still frustrating. As he cleared a room, he opened the windows wide to let as much fresh air in and nastiness out. *What is that smell?*

He suddenly was reminded of his youth, of being a young boy playing in his parents garage. They lived in a rural area and had many feral cats. It wasn't uncommon for a fox or coyote to injure one and have it crawl its way back home only to die in a back corner of the garage under a box. Then the heat of summer and the steady march of time would reveal the remains. Jake remembered finding one particularly bad one once and the stench of death was planted firmly in his memory. *Uh oh. Oh no! BILLIE!*

Jake rushed to his bedroom hoping for the best but trying to steel himself for the worst. The smell was almost overpowering, but Jake didn't even notice. He fell to his knees and wept. Billie, his beloved pet dog was dead. She was curled up in a ball on her doggie bed, eyes closed. It looked like she passed on while sleeping, *thank God for small graces,* he thought. He reached out and stroked her fur, she was cold but not stiff. A definite sign that she had been gone more than a day. The tears were flowing freely and fully now. He picked her up and held her, slowly rocking her back and forth.

"Jake?" Janey called out from the living room. She had gotten tired of waiting outside and had come in.

"In here." He croaked, his throat still tight. She appeared at the bedroom door and she instantly knew.

319

HOME BOUND

"Oh no!" She cried as she too began to cry for their lost pet. They sat and mourned for their lost beloved family member. Memories of her as a puppy frolicking in the yard and swimming at the beach flooded their minds. The loss was felt deeply for the couple.

When they had finally gotten themselves under control, Jake gently picked up his dog and carried her to the garage, Janey followed with her bed. Together they laid her down and covered her with a sheet. They held each other and cried some more. Billie had been their "first child", back when they had first been married. It would be hard on the kids since they had grown up with her being there.

"MOM? DAD? Is it safe to come in yet?" Joey yelled from the foyer. Jake stepped back and wiped away the tears, his eyes streaked red.

"Hold on a second!" He called back. "Come on, we have to get this house cleaned up and aired out. Then we will take care of her." Janey nodded and followed him out.

Jake gathered his new family outside and sat down on the front porch. They could tell that he had been crying and was still upset. He looked at his own kids and took a breath. It hitched in his throat as he spoke.

"I don't really know how to tell you this. Billie died. She must have died yesterday or the day before. She was in her bed, and it looks like she died in her sleep. So at least it was peaceful." Joey and Ella wailed for the loss of their furry sibling. Janey held Joey and Jake did the same with Ella, as they all cried. The rest of the group stared at the ground or the sky, anyplace but the weeping family. Jake cleared his throat and announced to the group.

"We have a lot of work to do to get the house back in shape after what Samantha and Billie did to it. After that we will have a funeral for her in the back yard. So let's shake this off, for now and get to it. Okay?" The scouts all nodded and quietly filed into the house, leaving the Hawkins family alone to grieve.

The scouts moved from room to room opening windows and cleaning up the leftover trash. They opened their water bottles and gave them to Samantha who lapped it up gratefully.

=================== * ===================

"The Hawkins family has taken a hit, but we are survivors. We can't have come this far only to fall. So let's brush ourselves off and keep moving forward. Okay?" Janey broke the silence and was the first to stand. She wiped away the tears and blew her nose with a tissue. Joey and Ella nodded.

"We all loved Billie but we still have Samantha and the hamsters to take care of, right?" Janey asked. The mention of their hamsters jolted them out of their melancholy malaise. The kids rushed into the house, straight to their rooms to check on their precious hamsters.

"Kenny is ok, but he needs food and water!" Joey called out from his room.

"Pajmina is ok too, and she needs food and water too!" Ella called from hers.

"Jake, I'm sure Samantha needs both too." Janey said softly.

"We already gave her some, Mrs. Hawkins." Answered one of the scouts from the open doorway. Jake smiled, nodded and thought for minute. He walked into the kitchen and called the scouts to him.

"Adam, Tim and Eric. Take this flashlight and go downstairs. Go with Mrs. Hawkins, she will show you where we store the water. Bring up two, three-gallon jugs and set them on the kitchen counter. Fill up your water bottles first then water the rest of the animals." He handed the boys a flashlight that he kept on the counter and they followed Janey downstairs. Jake watched them go, and then gathered up the soiled kitchen rugs.

Careful not to get any of the mess on himself, he took them outside and draped them over the fence.

He stood on his deck, closed his eyes, and took in a deep breath. He let it out slowly and calmly. He was home. *Be it ever so humble, there is no place like home!* He looked back inside and saw the kids working together to clean up his home. They were working together toward a new future. *My journey is over*, he thought, *but a new beginning is starting, at least I am HOME!*

THANK YOU FOR READING
HOME BOUND: A SURVIVAL STORY!

If you enjoyed it, I'd be eternally grateful if you would take a moment to write a short review (just a few words or maybe a bunch of words) and post it on Amazon. That sites uses complicated mathematics to determine what books are recommended to readers. By taking a few seconds to leave a review, you help me out and also help new readers learn about my work!

But before you leave...

Please check out the Hawkins Family Survival Stories Facebook page! Keep up with any new developments, get sneak peaks at upcoming chapters, be a part of the discussion and you might just find yourself in the novel!

Just search for: @HawkinsFamilySeries

Made in the USA
Las Vegas, NV
23 April 2021

21923977R00192